NURSE CALEY OF CASUALTY

On Barbara Caley's first shift in Casualty, Damien Elridge, a film star, and his fiancée Margaret Knowles are brought in from a car accident. Damien has promised Margaret a part in a film, but an argument before the crash has put both that and their prospective marriage into doubt — and when Damien meets Barbara, he immediately expresses an interest in her. But Barbara is already in love with Adam Thorne, the Casualty Officer, who is also Margaret's ex-fiancé. Can the quartet find their way through the tangle to happiness?

QUENNA TILBURY

NURSE CALEY OF CASUALTY

Complete and Unabridged

LINFORD
Leicester

First published in Great Britain in 1964

First Linford Edition
published 2019

A catalogue record for this book is available
from the British Library.

ISBN 978–1–4448–4196–1

Published by
F. A. Thorpe (Publishing)
Anstey, Leicestershire

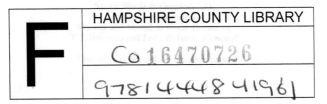

1

Barbara Caley straightened up and wiped the back of her hand across her forehead. Little beads of moisture clung to her honey-gold hair.

It was hot in the Casualty Hall, and her carefully set hair always rebelled during the hectic periods. The sleek shallow waves tightened up into the natural and rather childish bubble curls she strove so hard to banish. Honey-gold bubble curls and wide brown eyes gave her a childish look that didn't help to quell turbulent patients. It was an odd thing; one could keep the out-patients neatly regimented in their orderly rows outside each doctor's door, and it was easy enough to keep them moving neatly and quickly up as each patient went in, but, in the Casualty Hall, the patients were a law unto themselves.

By the very nature of their needs there could be no orderly treatment of them. Some crept in quietly with a hand or a leg or a head hastily bandaged with a handkerchief or any piece of cloth to hand. Some came in like a hurricane with the noisy heralding of the ambulance bells. To Barbara, a young nurse, doing her first turn on Casualty, that day had been a nightmare.

Even those who were used to it had to admit it had been quite a day in Casualty at the Hopwood General Hospital. After the long, hot August and the first two weeks of September, rain had set in, and the blistered roads had given in under the downpour. Every accident case who was in a condition to say anything blamed the surface of the roads and the teeming rain.

Everyone had something to say about the rain, when there was time to say anything. The nurses, the dressers, Casualty Sister, with her round, apple-rosy face and humorous grey eyes; the porters, the R.S.O. — the R.M.O. himself even — looked up occasionally to the glass squares in the ceiling, where the rain drummed unceasingly, and only the sullen, dark grey of the low skies could be seen.

The Casualty Officer alone worked grimly on, saying nothing about the weather. He was conspicuous among the Casualty staff for his size, the rough-hewn granite countenance that could, at times, look surprisingly tender, and the evenness of his temperament. In that part of the hospital where surprise was the main element, and speed the first essential, his even disposition was a godsend.

Adam Thorne had been born in Hopwood when it had been little more than a sprawling village. Most of his twenty-eight years had been spent pursuing a dream — the dream of his family as well as himself — of providing a hospital for the district.

The sale of the Thorne estate, on the death of his grandfather, had been the factor that had speeded up the family dream, for it had started the building of the many small houses so badly needed to accommodate the workers in the new factories.

Adam's aunt's house in the village had been the first cottage hospital, with a dozen beds. An uncle of his had been the founder of the present hospital; Thorne's Hospital it had been called in those days.

Now the sprawling new town of Hopwood, bristling with factories on each side of the river, had its own hospital, and its own place on the map. It was now important because of the new roundabout connecting two new trunk roads. Hopwood had arrived, but not as the Thorne family had envisaged it. Hopwood was fast becoming just another noisy, grimy, grey monster of a town, with more than its share of accidents to fill its new hospital.

'Help me over here, Nurse, please,' Adam Thorne said to Barbara, without looking at her.

4

He never looked at the faces of the nurses; he just raised his eyes half-way and took in the essential details of the uniform, to help with the correct appellation. Pale pink checks for student nurses, dark pink stripes for seniors. Brown belts for staff nurses. Grey dresses for the Sisters. A light mauve dress meant that he was speaking to an Assistant-Matron; purple meant Matron herself.

The faces didn't matter. No woman's face had meant anything to him since Margaret . . .

He pulled himself up sharply and concentrated on the little old lady he had asked the young nurse to help him with. He rarely let his thoughts slide back over the years in that way. It must be the rain. It had been drum-drumming that day — the day he most wished to forget.

'What happened — can you tell me?' he asked the patient gently, as he examined the limply hanging arm.

'I was hurrying for a bus,' the little

old lady said, with a rueful smile. 'My breathing's not so good as it was, Doctor, and my legs aren't so steady as they were. I slipped, and fell on the bus step. My arm took my whole weight. Ooh, that hurts!'

'Yes, I see. I'll try not to hurt too much. We'll get you along to be X-rayed. Nurse will help you,' and he fastened a sling round the injured arm as he spoke.

Barbara came forward and helped the old lady to her feet.

'Yes, Mr. Thorne,' she said. 'Now, Mrs. Drew, you come with me and I promise you it won't be half as bad as you think it will,' she said comfortingly to the patient.

She had a low, liquid, beautiful voice. The little old lady was delighted.

'Oh, you *are* a pretty little thing!' she said. 'Just like my little grand-daughter, all those fair curls and little doll face. What are you doing in a place like this, I should like to know?'

Adam Thorne did look up then,

mainly out of curiosity. The Casualty nurses were efficient, clean-looking, but he had never before heard a patient refer to one in such unusual terms. His own nurse, whom this new student was replacing, was more homely than the rest, but a tremendous prop to lean on. On the whole he felt he preferred reliability rather than prettiness.

His heart turned over as he caught a side view of Barbara's face as she helped the little old lady out of his room. She was so like Margaret.

He strode to the door to watch her progress but, as she turned to speak to a passing porter, he saw her full face and realised that she wasn't like Margaret at all really. Just that fleeting likeness side-face, and the colouring — that honey-gold hair, and the creamy skin. Smaller, too, than Margaret had been. Slighter in build. And much more pretty. No, she wasn't just pretty; she had a haunting loveliness. That beautiful speaking voice, too, and the glowing kindness in her smile . . .

He pulled himself up short, with surprise. This wasn't like him at all. Perhaps it meant that he was getting over losing Margaret. It was certainly the first time he had felt the slightest interest in any other woman.

He returned to his room and saw the next patient; a lad streaked with oil, from the factory across the way. He had caught his hand in a machine.

'You were fortunate, my lad,' Adam Thorne commented, as he examined the wound, 'to escape so lightly. Tell me, can you feel anything?'

'Oh, what are you pricking me for, doc? That didn't half hurt!'

'You're lucky. The nerve isn't damaged. How did it happen?'

'Search me, Doc! But don't tell me I'm lucky! Not me! To go and get this packet today of all days, I don't call that lucky! If anything's going to happen to me it's sure to be on a day I'm going out somewhere, or Christmas Day, or my birthday. Well, it's my birthday today! What a birthday!'

Adam Thorne smiled sympathetically and nodded, letting the lad's voice flow over his head while he thought of birthdays. It had been Margaret's birthday, that day, he recalled. Her birthday had been the factor that had started it all.

Margaret, her honey-gold hair freshly set, had been standing at the window of her aunt's home in Saxonbarn, when Adam had come round the back of the house that day. She hadn't been expecting him. He had been on call, and unexpectedly managed to exchange duties with someone else. It had been so important to him to wangle some free time to go and see her. In his pocket was the ring that was to make his engagement to Margaret official; his mother's ring, the one with the diamond cluster and the rubies, insured for a thousand pounds; the one Margaret had so much admired.

He had got off the bus before the regular stop in Saxonbarn and walked across the fields and through her aunt's orchard, to surprise Margaret. Never again would he try to give a woman a surprise. He had surprised her all right . . .

Dragging his mind back again he finished the routine dressing and dismissed the lad.

Barbara Caley came back, all apologies.

'I'm sorry I've been so long, Mr. Thorne, but she was so scared of the X-ray machine when she saw it through an open door that I stayed with her till she went in. Was it all right?'

'Quite all right, Nurse,' he said, looking at her again. 'A few minutes spent on giving the patient confidence is not time wasted, in my opinion.'

His words chased the anxiety from her face and that lovely smile broke out again, like sudden sunshine through clouds.

'Oh, thank you,' she said, with a rush, and turned to help him with the next patient.

They were all piling up again. A little

girl who had disobeyed her mother and gone on to a main road with her small bike; badly frightened still at being caught in the sudden holding up of the press of traffic, a tall removal van in front of her, a lorry and a bus behind and, panicking, she had fallen off, but had been dragged clear by a passerby, with no more than cuts and bruises for her folly. Barbara cuddled her and chased the tears away by telling her about her own exploits on her first fairy cycle and what a mess she had made of trying to ride.

Then there was the crossing-sweeper who had slipped on the greasy road, in front of a milk float; the window cleaner, used to climbing great heights and coming to no harm, had been forced to do an inside job because of the rain, and had put his hand through a pane of glass.

On and on they came, in a never-ceasing flow, until at last Casualty Sister came and sent Barbara off to her lunch.

In the big dining-hall she had found Sue Gardner, who had begun training the same day as she had, and who had worked side by side with Barbara until the last General Post. Sue, to her great delight, had been sent to the Maternity Wing. Sue loved babies.

'Lucky for you, you didn't get sent to Casualty,' Barbara commented, pushing her cap back and starting on her mutton stew and peas with gusto. 'It's awful! The only thing it does for you is to make you hungry; it makes you even want to eat mutton stew.'

'What's the Casualty Officer like?' That was all Sue wanted to know. 'Everyone's talking about him on Maternity. They say he doesn't really look at you because of his sad past. Honestly! How corny can you get?'

'Well, he doesn't really, but I think it's only because he's so interested in the patients that he doesn't know the nurses exist. Can you blame him? It was my first day and I felt so ham-fisted, I might have had footballs

12

instead of hands. I must have irritated him, but he's so kind. Rather sweet, really.'

'Golly! That must be the effect that baby face of yours has on him!' Sue said, admiringly. She was little and dark and tough and wiry, peppered with freckles, and a pair of wicked, darting green eyes that made the staider ward sisters tremble. If there was nonsense going on in the wards it was bound to be Sue at the bottom of it.

'Why do they talk about him in Maternity?' Barbara wanted to know.

'Some of the mothers remember him,' Sue said, thoughtfully, 'as a fifth year medical student doing his midwifery course. They're very romantic at heart and sorry for him because his love affair went wrong. Actually, if it's true, then it's rather a shame. But you know how everyone exaggerates in this place. It seems he was practically engaged to a girl who lives in that big house on the London road, just beyond the new by-pass. It used to be all country there and the Casualty Officer walked across the fields to go in the back way one day and caught her telephoning some other fellow. It must have been an awful shock to him.'

'How did he know it was some other man?' Barbara asked, finishing the stew with satisfaction and turning her thoughts to the jam tart and custard.

'That's what puzzled me at first but it seems that his family and hers were old friends — well, her aunt and his grandmother — and he was used to drifting in and out of the back way if he felt like it. This girl, Margaret Knowles, thought he was on call (and he was, too, only at the last minute he managed to swap duties with someone) so she wasn't expecting him. The telephone started to ring as he was crossing the hall and he picked it up but she picked up the extension in her bedroom, and started to talk before he could say anything. From what little he listened to he gathered they'd known each other for some time and were planning to tell

14

Adam Thorne that it was all off.'

'Oh, I say! How ghastly!' Barbara exclaimed, thinking of that kindly face, with its controlled expression, and the sensitive hands that probed so delicately over the hurt areas of damaged bodies that morning. 'How could she do it to him? What was the other man like?'

'This'll surprise you,' Sue said with satisfaction. She didn't know Adam Thorne, she hadn't even met him, and she was enjoying the telling of a story about a stranger. 'Remember that actor we saw in the film at the Regal last week?'

Barbara thought. 'Damien Eldridge? Not him!'

'That's right. Well, I suppose you can't blame someone for falling for someone like him — a film star, I mean — instead of a Casualty Officer in a place like this? I mean to say! Well, wouldn't you prefer Damien Eldridge?'

Barbara ate jam tart thoughtfully. 'I couldn't do it to him,' she said at last.

'He's, well, he's not the sort of man I could do that to, ever. Not that I could break an engagement, anyway.'

'But they weren't officially engaged,' Sue remarked.

She thought of the Casualty Officer as someone as anonymous as the back of a spoon. She hadn't even seen him. But she knew every feature of Damien Eldridge's face, close-up; knew his voice, had succumbed to his charm through five different films, for most of which she had queued in the rain, or stood melting in the heat. Damien Eldridge was, for her, a real person; the sort of man a girl dreams about.

'Just the same,' Barbara insisted, 'when you've met him you'll see what I mean. It was a horrible thing to do.'

'Bar, you haven't fallen for him — not after just one morning in Casualty!' Sue was frankly scandalised.

'Don't be silly, of course I haven't,' Barbara refuted. 'But he's terribly nice. I was a long time taking a patient down to X-ray and, instead of bawling me out, what do you think he said? 'Time spent on giving a patient confidence isn't time wasted'. How's that for being nice to a mere student nurse? Can you see Dr. Bushell or the R.S.O. doing that, because I can't!'

'All right,' Sue gurgled, 'so the Casualty Officer's nice. Humane to dumb student nurses. But that doesn't make him more acceptable in marriage than Damien Eldridge, and you can't say it does.'

'I know that, Sue, but isn't it a question of trusting someone? I mean, supposing you were about to be engaged to, well, Colin Price, for instance. Well, you do rather like him, don't you? And, supposing you found he was thinking of jilting you for someone terribly glamorous — a film actress, say? Wouldn't you be fed up about it? It wouldn't be honest, would it?'

'Yes, I suppose you're right,' Sue agreed. 'But don't go all mushy about the Casualty Officer on the strength of it when you get back to Casualty this afternoon!' she warned.

'As if there'll be time,' Barbara replied, finishing her tart with an eye on the clock. 'I have never seen so many patients all wanting attention at once. No one has time to *breathe*!'

She hurried down to the Casualty Hall again and found Adam Thorne was at lunch. Colin Price, the medical student Sue was going around with at that time, was in Adam Thorne's room, doing the small cuts and queries.

'Hallo, Bar!' he said, cheerily. 'This your first day down here? How do you find it?'

'Terrifying!' Barbara said, promptly. 'I don't think I could bear it if Mr. Thorne weren't so understanding.'

Colin blinked. 'Understanding! That's a new one! Oh, well, I suppose his Nibs *would* be like that with you! It's that innocent, child look of yours, I suppose. So long as he doesn't realise you're as wicked as any other student nurse, you'll be all right!'

'How can you say such a thing?' she protested. 'It's not like that at all.'

'Well, watch out, that's all! He was crossed in love and women scare the daylights out of him. I'm telling you!'

All the time he was talking he was probing at a small boy's hand. He worried Barbara because of his way of exchanging jolly conversation with other people while he appeared to be giving only half of his attention to the patient.

'Can I help?' she asked him anxiously.

'Oh, heavens, no! We're having a lovely time with a deep-seated splinter. Can't think how this chap got it in so far. Buried it on purpose, I shouldn't wonder, eh, fella?'

The grubby boy of nine grinned back in great humour. He, at least, wholly approved of Colin's performance.

Between them, Barbara and Colin had polished off six more routine cases when Adam Thorne came back. As he came into the room and took over from

Colin he looked at Barbara, and she found those deep-set eyes of his rather disconcerting. She found herself thinking that she wouldn't like to be in the shoes of that girl who had jilted him.

'They tell me it's your first day down here,' Adam Thorne said, unexpectedly. 'I hope this morning didn't put you off. It isn't always like that. Perhaps we shall have a quieter afternoon.'

But, even as he spoke, they heard the clamour of ambulance bells. Another big accident.

This accident was indeed sufficiently big enough to bring down from the wards anyone who was free to help. The R.S.O. came through, his white coat flying out behind him. He had just been taking it off to go off duty and had hastily put it on again.

Some of the students, in their resident period before exams, gladly came, for the extra experience. The R.M.O. appeared and with him Sir Percy — still at the hospital because of a patient admitted the day before about whom he wasn't happy. Sir Percy hadn't got a home, the nursing staff said irreverently among themselves. It wasn't that they didn't like him, nor that they were unaware that he had not only a home but a large and well-run staff and a great deal more comfort than Mr. Rudd or Sir Noel. No, it was just that Sir Percy loved his work and seized any excuse to stay on when he should long ago have been seen off the premises.

Now he came in rubbing his hands just as if, another student said witheringly in an aside to Barbara as she fled by, he enjoyed a full-scale accident.

The porters were dashing about, wheeling empty stretcher trolleys, moving in slowly and carefully with loaded ones. Casualty had again sprung to life, just when it was beginning to get a bit quiet, Barbara thought, as she helped a woman with a torn dress and a half-empty shopping basket, into a cubicle and began to take down her particulars.

The woman was half crying, half gasping, and very worried about her purchases.

'Lost half of them and my purse has gone into the river!' she kept saying, over and over again. 'But I did hang on to my boy's raincoat. Can't afford to lose that! Where is my boy? He'll be soaking wet in this rain! I can't get him new clothes because my purse went into the river — I saw it go so I know I've lost it.'

Colin Price, so lately laughing and chatting over the other lad's splinter, came in with a grave face and began to examine her.

'She won't need that raincoat,' he said, in a low voice to Barbara. 'Stay with her. I'll be back.'

The bus on which the woman had been travelling had skidded at the corner of the bridge in trying to avoid a large private car, and had crashed through the stone parapet. The bus had then remained suspended. Already cranes and tackle were on the spot, endeavouring to clear it, to open the bridge again for traffic.

'What happened to the car?' Barbara heard Colin Price ask someone else as she went up to the wards with the patient.

Walking soberly beside the stretcher Barbara saw the rest of the shoppers from the crowded bus. Some were just suffering from shock and would be allowed to go home. Most of them had bandages somewhere; heads, arms, and one man had his face almost entirely covered. A nurse was helping him across Casualty Hall. He hardly knew where he was going.

Someone had supplied the answer regarding the car. It had gone through the open window of an ironmonger's shop. The passenger was quite well known.

'Damien Eldridge, that film actor who was over at Maplefield to open the Flower Show,' one of the porters muttered to the other.

Barbara's legs felt wobbly as she

caught the words. She hadn't even known he was in the district. She felt dreadful, as if it was someone she really knew who had been hurt. Like Sue, she felt that she really knew him from having seen him so often on the screen.

She wanted to ask if he were badly hurt, but her throat felt dry and peculiar. She kept thinking about that girl, Margaret Knowles, who had thrown over nice Adam Thorne, for the film star. What would she feel when she heard the news? Where was she, while he was opening the Flower Show? Here — at her home? So little had been said about where she was, or what she did with herself all day long, since she had become the fiancée of a film star.

'Who was driving, then?' the other porter asked. 'Does he have a chauffeur?'

'No, that's the funny thing. It was a young lady driving him, and a right mess she's in, they say. They haven't brought her in yet. She was still trapped in the car but he seems to have got off fairly lightly.'

Barbara was conscious of a wave of relief. He wasn't hurt too badly. That handsome, charming, smiling face wasn't marked, or they would have said so.

Sister claimed Barbara, when she returned, to help the R.S.O. do a minor op. at the end. Then Barbara was working beside Adam Thorne, holding the head of a young girl while her eye was being dressed.

One after another, they were clearing the Hall again. Here a drip to be set up, there a sleeve to be cut away where the arm was too damaged to risk disturbing it too much.

Between patients, Barbara paused to think of the girl driver of the film star's car. It wasn't all fun to work for someone like Damien Eldridge, if it meant getting badly hurt at the wheel of his car, she remembered thinking.

Then the last ambulance came in and Adam Thorne went out to meet it.

Barbara hurried along behind him, in an effort to keep up with those long strides of his.

She felt peculiar. Sue had said, before she came on duty this morning, that this was to be a testing time. In the year they had been at the hospital Barbara found that she was the one who suffered with the patients; the one who cared too much about them and got hurt too badly. Sue took it all in her stride, sympathising without sustaining hurt herself. Casualty duty was to be the test. If she couldn't stand up to the sight of so much blood, so many injuries, she would give up nursing, she had said.

Now, after a hectic day of it, she wondered whether she could go on. This must be the girl driver of the film star's car, and she shrank from looking but forced herself to do so.

Adam Thorne was beside the stretcher, lifting the blanket. Barbara watched his face so that she shouldn't look at the girl too soon. Watching him, she took the full brunt of the shock. He stared, unbelieving, his face slowly whitening to the lips. He looked as if he had been dealt a mortal blow. The porters handling the stretcher looked sharply at him. It seemed to Barbara that he even swayed a little. Then he took hold of himself with what seemed a super-human effort, and went inside again beside the stretcher. But before he did so he uttered one word beneath his breath, and only Barbara caught it.

'*Margaret!*' she thought she heard him say.

2

It was a terrible shock to everyone. In the strange way that the grapevine works word flashed round in no time that the latest — and perhaps the worst — casualty to be brought in was the one-time fiancée of Adam Thorne.

Adam's own nurse had come back and was working with him. Barbara was sent down to the end to help with the minor casualties still arriving. She was deeply grateful for that. She didn't want to have to be the one to help him with that girl's broken body. The memory of his face, when he looked down at the girl, was one that would haunt her for a long time, Barbara felt.

Yet Adam Thorne had himself well under control after that first lapse. He treated the girl as quietly and kindly as if she were a complete stranger to him.

In no time at all Margaret Knowles

was taken up to the theatre. A small private ward was prepared for her. Casualty settled down to the rather slower trickle of local and domestic accidents, as if the big accident had never happened.

When Barbara went off duty that night Sue was full of the accident. 'Can you beat it? We were only talking about Damien Eldridge today and then he gets brought into the hospital!'

'It was horrible!' Barbara said, in a heartfelt tone. 'I didn't see him myself. I only saw that girl.'

She described the scene. It was vividly stamped on her mind.

'That's another thing everyone's talking about,' Sue exclaimed. 'Did Adam Thorne say anything about her?'

'No, not a thing. He looked perfectly ghastly for a minute or two. I thought he was going to pass out. Then he seemed to pull himself together and he went on just as if she was someone he didn't even know. How can anyone do that?'

'I heard two senior nurses talking about it and they were saying it's typical of him. He's too proud to let people see what he's feeling. Besides, he says it's bad for the department, so they were saying. Wonder what sort of man he is?'

'Rather super sort of person, I should think,' Barbara said softly, remembering. 'But not one I'd like in the family. I'd feel I was falling so short of his standards that I'd always have a guilt complex.'

'Me, too,' Sue said, fervently. 'Give me Damien Eldridge every time. Would you like to see him?' she asked, suddenly.

'See him! I'd love to. But how would it be possible? I expect he's in a private room. He wouldn't be on the wards.'

'That's just it,' Sue said excitedly. 'Remember my Uncle James? He's back again in Men's Surgical — his leg's playing him up again. I promised I'd go up and see him tomorrow. Want to come?'

'I'd like to see your uncle again, Sue.

He's a dear. But I can't see how we'll get a glimpse of Damien Eldridge.'

'We might — we might not. But at least we'll hear all about it from Uncle James. Nurse Beck's on his ward and she told me he's just inside and he's got an excellent view of the door of the first side ward where Damien is. Uncle was always lucky. From that position he can see most of the comings and goings of everyone. There have been masses of flowers and presents go up and the Press has been there already.'

'What did Damien Eldridge get in the way of injuries?' Barbara asked in a muffled voice, almost afraid to hear the answer.

'Just a bash on the legs, I think. Wouldn't it have been awful if he'd got his face messed up? Honestly, I don't think I've ever seen such a good-looking man. They say he's awfully kind to young actresses just starting — helpful and all that. Absolutely no side at all. The nurses and the porters — even Sister! — adore him already. Wish we could meet him.'

A warm little glow filled Barbara. 'Me, too,' she said. 'Funny, isn't it? After all the times we've queued in the hope of getting a glimpse of him when he's been making a personal appearance, and it has to be here in the hospital that we might get that chance after all!'

'Wonder why he wasn't driving the car, though?' Sue murmured. 'It was a blessing in disguise that he wasn't, wasn't it? Well, I mean, one has to be realistic and his career might have been ruined if he'd been in the driving seat. He wouldn't have escaped so lightly.'

'I heard a policeman say that they thought it was partly his driver's fault and partly the bus driver's. It shakes you, doesn't it — something happening like that right on your own doorstep.'

In a place where accidents were the order of the day, this accident was outstanding. Damien Eldridge had been opening a local flower show. He had been standing in for some other film star in his own company who was unable to do the job, otherwise he would have been nowhere near Hopwood at that time. Margaret Knowles' aunt's home was just outside Hopwood but she rarely went there. She hadn't been home since she had jilted the Casualty Officer. Yet it had to be here that they had both been caught on their way back to London. It was like the workings of fate, Barbara thought.

What would he be like, now he was stripped of all his glamour, reduced to being just one patient of many in a white enamelled bed in the small bare room just outside Men's Surgical? Would he appear as good-looking and charming, she wondered?

In spite of herself she couldn't keep down her excitement the next day, as she worked through the morning and looked forward to the afternoon, the week-end visiting time.

Casualty was no more quiet on a Sunday than at any other time. True, since the factories were closed, there were no hands caught in machines, but there were plenty of home accidents; burns and scalds while preparing Sunday dinner, and the accidents to enthusiastic car and motor-cycle owners taking the morning to clean their vehicles. There were still the usual number of old people falling downstairs, and children swallowing foreign bodies. There were still casualties on the road.

Yet there was an air of Sunday calm in spite of all that and when Barbara went off duty in the afternoon, she felt a lightening of the gloom she had experienced yesterday. This was no longer her first day in Casualty. Casualty wasn't half a bad place, she felt.

Sue was bubbling with high spirits. Not only was there the possibility of a view of the film star but twins had been born in the small hours in the Maternity Wing — Sue's first experience of new-born twins.

Sue's Uncle James didn't share their

enthusiasm, either about the new babies or about the film star. For him, the interest lay in the enterprising camera-man who had tried to gate-crash the ward in search of a pretty nurse to stand over the film star for the picture he was taking.

'You two should have been around,' James Gardner chuckled. 'The answer to a camera-man's prayer — especially young Barbara here. You're too pretty to be a nurse, young woman!'

'Oh, how you do run on, Mr. Gardner,' Barbara scolded. 'Never mind that — what did the Sister say, or didn't she know about it?'

'Ah, I'm coming to that! She's only a little scrap, you know, and he was a big chap, but she shoo-ed him and his camera out of the place in double quick time! Was she furious — and indignant! Intruding on her ward without permission! She absolutely shook with rage. It was worth seeing, I can assure you.'

People still came and went from the private room. Sue said wistfully; 'Couldn't we pretend we had an important message for him, to get us in there? Who'd know?'

'What d'you want to see him for? You can see him on the pictures any day,' Sue's uncle remarked.

'That's not the point, Uncle, and you know it!' Sue retorted. 'We want to see him in the flesh.'

'Well, I don't suppose you will. All the nurses on this ward have been threatened with dire consequences if they try to get in there without good (and official) reasons. Sister's said he's a patient like everyone else and she's not going to have him bothered by silly girls staring at him. I heard her say it myself — so I wouldn't advise you two to take any chances.'

As it happened they didn't have to. Damien Eldridge was being wheeled out to the bathrom in a chair as they left Men's Surgical.

They stood back to let him go past them. His leg was strapped to a splint, out stiff before him, but otherwise he didn't look too bad.

He smiled at them. That quick, brilliant smile they both knew so well. He was really incredibly good-looking. The clean line of nose and jaw, the beautifully moulded cheek-bones and forehead, the almost pretty ears, and the unusual hair-line of light brown hair, all made up a distinctive face which lifted him above the ranks of the many good-looking young men on the screen.

Just that glimpse of him was a thrill but, as he passed them, he tried to turn round to look at them again, and it was Barbara he looked at.

The Staff-Nurse — one of the plain, efficient ones the hospital abounded in — said something to him and he looked ahead again, but the two girls had caught the little action. Sue squeezed Barbara's arm and said, 'He *looked* at you! D'you realise — he *looked* at you!'

'Much good may it do me,' Barbara retorted, as they hurried down the corridor.

'He's marvellous,' Sue breathed. 'Honestly, you must admit that the men in our lives are pretty ordinary in comparison! Wonder what it's like to work on the films and meet people like that every day! I don't care what anyone says about being a dedicated nurse and just adoring to treat sick people — it does you good, to come across someone like Damien Eldridge!'

'Better not let Sister Tutor hear you say that, Sue!'

'Oh, I know she says we must love the patients, but how can you. Oh, most of my little mothers are pets, but they're women, and they've all got a man in their lives, and bless us, there's precious little glamour about their men either from what I can hear of it. Bar, don't you just *wish* you could have a bit of glamour, just once, before one gets set in one's ways? Just one little period in one's life with lovely people, and nice things, to look back on, I mean?'

Barbara laughed at her friend. 'He's turned your head, just one glimpse of him in a chair being wheeled to the bathroom — oh, Sue!'

'I know that wasn't very glamorous but still, it just shows how marvellous he is, that he could still look super under those conditions, with a splint on his leg, too.'

'Yes, I know what you mean. Actually, what struck me was not his glamour so much as the fact that he looks so nice. Really nice, I mean. I was thinking, how could such a nice person do that to Adam Thorne — stealing his fiancée? I mean, it wouldn't have been so bad if it had been all out in the open but, from what I've heard about it, it was rather underhanded, the way it was done. D'you see what I mean?'

Sue looked troubled. 'I thought of that, too,' she admitted, unwilling even now to drag her idol down off his pedestal. 'Still, gossip distorts everything. We've heard what everyone says, but we don't know the inside story. What's Adam Thorne like? I mean, would he be the sort not to see that kind of thing going on under his very nose?' She looked very seriously at her friend. 'Who would you rather marry, Bar — someone like the Casualty Officer or Damien Eldridge? I think I know which one I'd choose, the same as that girl did.'

'That girl — Margaret Knowles. What's it like lying there all alone?' Barbara mused. 'I wonder if she had time to realise that she was causing an accident, or whether she was so engrossed in talking to Damien Eldridge, that she just never saw what hit her? They say she was actually looking at him and saying something to him — think of it, taking your eyes off the road when you're driving!'

'Wonder if they've told her he got hurt too? Or if she thinks he's dead?' Sue said, thinking aloud.

★   ★   ★

Adam went up to Margaret's room every day. The hospital buzzed with rumours. Would they come together again? Was he still in love with Margaret, or merely paying a duty visit? And how much of the accident had she been told?

Barbara saw Margaret's aunt go up one day. She was a tall, upright, elderly woman with an air of distinction that made Barbara wonder if Margaret had been like that. The junior who 'special-led' Margaret Knowles had said that she wasn't good-looking at all, and what could be seen of her face made one wonder what Damien Eldridge had seen in her.

One day Adam Thorne couldn't get up to Margaret's room to make his daily visit.

Barbara was just going off duty and saw him ripping off his coat. In the other hand he was trying to balance some books, and off the top of the pile an exquisite basket of fruit was gently sliding. She moved forward and saved it just in time.

'Can I help you, Mr. Thorne?' she

asked him. He looked very worried, unusually so.

'Actually I wanted to take these up to Miss Knowles,' he admitted, 'but I've got an important appointment. I wonder if you'd mind taking them up to her when you go off duty?'

'Of course I will,' Barbara told him.

'And this letter,' he said, looking at his watch. 'Tell her why I couldn't come, will you, I don't want her to think — oh, I must dash. Thanks a lot, Nurse.'

He smiled at her, that sweet smile that crinkled his face, before he hurried out to his car.

Barbara took the pile of things up and spoke to the Staff Nurse in charge. She was aware that she was holding her breath in sheer anticipation. Now she would see Margaret Knowles at close quarters . . . the girl who could still claim all this devotion from Adam Thorne although she had treated him so shabbily not so long ago. This was the girl who could also claim the attentions of someone as sought-after as Damien Eldridge.

'Are you asleep, dear?' Staff Nurse said brightly to the girl in the bed. 'Mr. Thorne couldn't manage to come up so he asked his nurse to bring some things for you. She wants to say hallo to you.'

The girl rolled her head over and looked up at the Staff Nurse's thin, dark face with its no-nonsense smile. Then she slid her eyes away to seek those of Barbara. The Staff Nurse, with a brief smile and nod, rustled out, leaving them alone together. Margaret went on staring.

Barbara caught her breath for an instant. So this was what the little nurse had meant! Margaret Knowles' face was half covered with cuts, which were being healed by the open method. A bandage was round her head and some of the honey-gold hair escaped at the back. If she had ever been attractive her good looks had all gone now.

Barbara's heart ached for her. She smiled — perhaps more warmly than she had intended. She didn't know it but her vivid young face and glorious colouring hurt the girl in the bed far more than the absence of a favourite visitor could have done.

'Hallo,' Barbara said, still smiling. 'Do you feel like a bit of a chat, or shall I just dump these and go?'

'Stay, if you please,' Margaret said. Her mouth hardly moved because of her swollen and bruised lips. Her speech sounded slurred, and her voice — always rather husky — was now frankly indistinct. 'Show me!'

Barbara held each book up for her to see and also the fruit.

Margaret had little interest in any of them. It was the letter from Adam that caught her attention.

'Shall I open it for you?' Barbara asked, sitting on the chair by her bedside. 'Then you can read it if I hold it up, can't you?'

'Yes, open it,' Margaret instructed, never taking her eyes off Barbara. Then, quite suddenly she said, 'You're the same colouring as I am. Pretty, too, like I used to be.'

It shocked Barbara so much that she couldn't hold on to the smile. She could feel her face freezing but she made the effort to give the comfort the patient required.

'You can't expect to feel glamorous in bed after what you've been through,' she said, gently, 'but you'll be all right when you're well!'

The swollen lips parted in an awful travesty of a smile. 'You sound just like Adam Thorne. Well, let's hear what he says. Read his letter out loud to me, will you?'

3

This was a thing Barbara had never had to do before. She had read family letters, to Grans and to children, and to the odd patient whose sight was defective, but never a love letter — and that was what Adam Thorne's letter might well turn out to be, she told herself.

But the patient was insisting, nodding her head repeatedly, so, with heightened colour, Barbara read:

'Margo, dearest, I am in a flat spin today and have to go in a great hurry to Larksgate, but don't worry, I'll be up to see you tomorrow. Remember all the things I said to you yesterday, and hang on, my dear girl — I promise you I'll see you through. Adam.'

There was a little silence; then Margaret said, 'Thank you, Nurse. Are there any other letters?'

'No, I'm afraid there's no more post today,' Barbara said, folding the letter with fingers clumsy with embarrassment and putting it back into the envelope. To Sue that letter would have presented no difficulties, but to Barbara it was like opening a door of a private room and peeping in. From what she knew of Adam Thorne, from all she had heard said of him and that old love affair, he would be the last person to relish his letter being read by the nurse who worked with him.

Margaret didn't seem to mind one way or the other.

'I didn't mean post. I meant ... anyone in the hospital. Damien Eldridge, for instance.'

She watched Barbara closely as she waited for her answer.

'I'm sorry but I haven't anything from him for you. It was Mr. Thorne who gave me these things. I work down in Casualty with him, you see. I happened to be handy and not doing anything.'

'I see. Damien Eldridge — they say he wasn't badly hurt. Is that true? Have you seen him?'

'I did see him being wheeled up the corridor to the bathroom,' Barbara said, carefully. She hadn't been briefed on how much to disclose to the patient but there surely couldn't be any harm in that.

'Does he know — about me?' Margaret enquired.

'I've no idea,' Barbara said, getting up to go.

'Please don't go — unless you're in a hurry,' Margaret pleaded. 'No one else stays to talk to me. Only Adam and he just gives me a pep-talk. I don't want a pep-talk. I want the truth.'

She moved restlessly, so Barbara sat down again.

'I feel frightfully weak and I keep feeling that I'm not going to get about again. It's my legs. Damien likes to keep on the move. He gets bored if he can't. They say I shall have to rest for ages. Damien will want to keep going and he won't want me any more. Have you any idea what it's like to be engaged to a film star?'

'No, I'm afraid I haven't. But I expect it's a very exciting life, isn't it?' Barbara said.

'Oh, it's exciting all right.' A spark of life came into Margaret's pale blue eyes. 'I'm going to have a screen test. Did you know that? Oh, yes, Damien's going to arrange it for me.'

Barbara felt the smile again freezing on her face. But she had to try to keep on smiling for fear a look of horror should take the place of it. The poignancy of that moment brought a lump into her throat, for, clearly, Margaret had no idea what her face looked like.

'How thrilling!' Barbara exclaimed, at a loss to know what to say. 'I wonder what it's like to be in the film world? Do you watch Mr. Eldridge at work on the set?'

She couldn't have chosen a better opening. Warmth crept into Margaret's voice as she answered.

'Oh, yes. I'm with him all the time he's at the studios. I help him with his lines, too, and I'm in at all the discussions, about make-up and costume, and production details. Then there are the parties — oh, those parties! How I'm going to miss them, lying here. You've no idea, Nurse, what a bore it's going to be, after the life Damien and I enjoy.'

Sister came in at that moment and, after a brief glance at the patient, she looked pleased.

'Having a little chat, dear? That's nice. But I think Nurse had better go now. We mustn't allow you to tire yourself, must we, or we shall have Mr. Thorne after us!'

'Oh, must she go?' Margaret protested. 'But she can come again, can't she? You will come again, Nurse, won't you? I have enjoyed our chat.'

'Yes, Nurse may visit you again if she wishes,' Sister said slowly, looking at Barbara thoughtfully.

'I'd like to very much, Sister, if I may,' Barbara said, warmly. It was heartening to find that she could reach out to someone as difficult as this patient, after the rather unpromising beginning.

'Then that's settled. Just come up when you're free, Nurse, but make the visits short, for the time being, at any-rate,' Sister said.

Barbara opened the door for her to go out and held it open. She waved to Margaret as she slipped out and found Sister waiting for her in the corridor.

'The patient looks better. Nurse. That was kind of you,' Sister said, approvingly.

'It wasn't my idea, Sister,' Barbara hastened to explain. 'Mr. Thorne couldn't come and he asked me to bring a few things from him and to say why he couldn't visit her himself. Then she wanted to talk.'

Sister nodded. 'We haven't been able to get her to make such an effort so far.

What did you find to talk about?'

Barbara looked rather uncomfortable.

'She wanted to discuss Mr. Eldridge,' she said, 'and working with him. She's anxious to get back — she was to have a part in a film. Was it all right to let her talk about that, Sister?'

'Yes, of course, if she wants to, Nurse, so long as you didn't let her know how long it would be before she could hope to think of such a thing again — if ever.'

Barbara's eyes misted. 'No, I didn't let her know, Sister. I realised she doesn't seem to know about her face. Suppose she gets hold of a mirror one day?'

'That is the one thing we have to guard against for the time being,' Sister said, briskly.

She dismissed Barbara then but there was no doubt that Sister Henty was very much pleased with Barbara's visit and the effect on the patient.

Barbara didn't see the Casualty

Officer again until the next day. He looked up when she passed the open door of his little room and called to her.

'Thank you, Nurse, for going to see Miss Knowles for me. Sister tells me she seems much brighter.'

'I'm so glad,' Barbara said, hoping he wouldn't say any more. She didn't want him to know that she had read his letter aloud to Margaret.

He seemed at a loss to know how to put what he had to say into words. After a pause he said, feeling his way, 'She looked rather like you — as to height and colouring, you know — before the accident. Did she, by any chance, mention that?'

'Yes, she did, but she talked mainly about her future in pictures.'

He shot his head up at that, his eyes one big question.

'She doesn't appear to know what her face is like,' Barbara said, quickly. 'I was afraid she would ask about her injuries so I encouraged her to tell me about her life in the film world, and she seemed to forget about her present condition.'

'Good girl,' he approved. 'Sister tells me that Miss Knowles asked to see you again. I'd be very grateful if you could spare a minute or two. You've achieved a minor miracle.'

Barbara smiled faintly and got away as soon as she could reasonably escape. She didn't think it would be a good move to tell him that the thought of Damien Eldridge had lighted the spark which had really set the patient going — and not anything that Barbara herself had done.

She did go up again the following day. Her off-duty hours no longer coincided with Adam Thorne's so she could be reasonably sure of picking a time when the patient would be alone.

There had been a different bandage put on Margaret's head. It showed more of her hair which had been hastily cut short and looked unprepossessing. Margaret, too, was the sort of girl who looked woefully undressed without complete facial make-up. She was fretting for her make-up case, she told Barbara, almost before Barbara had time to say hallo and sit down by the bed.

'Well,' Barbara confided, 'actually the nursing staff don't like the patients to use much make-up. It makes the pillow-cases messy and it never stays right in bed. So you're probably pleasing everyone by not using make-up just yet.'

'I must look awful without it! I feel so undressed! Supposing Damien came to see me? He's never seen me without make-up.'

She looked appalled at the idea and Barbara's face was glum, too, but for a different reason. She had no idea how Damien Eldridge would take the sight of his once-attractive fiancée with the uncovered cuts on her face.

'I don't think you need fear his coming on you without warning,' Barbara hastened to say. 'You see, he is allowed to go to the bathroom but that's the lot for the moment. Because of the distance between Men's Surgical and here,' she added, hastily. One had to be so careful how much to let the patient know, or she'd be worrying about his injuries next.

'Are you sure?' Margaret asked, anxiously. 'That he won't take me by surprise, I mean? I haven't anything really pretty to wear, either. Look at me! What a dreary sight I must look in these hospital clothes. I say, do you think you could get someone to go to my room at home and bring some of my nice things to wear? Could you go yourself — when you go off duty?'

'Yes, I don't mind,' Barbara agreed readily. 'If you give me your aunt's telephone number I could ask her to get some things ready for me in a case. Then I'd only have to pick it up.'

Margaret moved restlessly. 'That isn't what I said. If I'd wanted my aunt to do it I could ask her when she comes herself. No, I want you to go to my room. Tell her I asked you to. And you pick some really nice things. My aunt has the old-fashioned idea that one shouldn't wear fussy things in hospital. She doesn't approve of half the clothes I wear, anyway, and I believe she thinks my underwear is frankly sinful!'

A brief smile tore at her face. It obviously caused her pain to smile, so she let it slide away and a puzzled frown took its place. 'My face hurts! Why? What's the matter with it? Have they done anything to it without telling me?'

'Take it easy,' Barbara said, quietly. 'Just think — you've been badly shaken up and you're bound to feel odd aches and pains that you never noticed before. That's only sense, isn't it?'

Margaret looked doubtful, and then relieved.

'Oh, yes, I suppose so, after that crash.'

'I dare say your fiancé will be complaining of new bruises pretty soon. It's reaction that sets in, you know,' Barbara added, partly to soothe her, partly to sound her out, in order to see how much she really knew about Damien's condition.

'Oh, him! He's a fool! It was his fault that I — well, if he'd let me do what I wanted to, I'd never have — ' and again she broke off, staring at the ceiling, angry glints in her eyes. 'The trouble is, he's afraid I shall become a great actress, and *he* wants to be top all the time.'

Barbara was shocked. Usually patients discovered how much they loved the people close to them when they were helpless in bed. But this girl didn't appear to love Damien so much as to value his place in life and the importance of the connection with him. Or was this resentful attitude part of the aftermath of the accident? Barbara couldn't help feeling that if it weren't, and it was Margaret's natural disposition to be so scathing about those close to her, then Adam Thorne had had a happy escape when she had jilted him.

The silence penetrated to Margaret.

She turned her head sharply, the angry look disappearing.

'Oh, hark at me!' she said. 'Don't take any notice of me. It isn't like that really. I don't mean that at all. What must you be thinking? I don't really think those things about him — it's just that I'm lying here, helpless, telling myself that it was his fault, but it wasn't. It was mine!'

'Oh, don't think about it,' Barbara urged, compassion taking the place of her former anger. In such a dreadful situation what would she herself be thinking? Probably the same sort of things.

'But I must. I think about it all the time. I can't stop thinking about it. I lie here at night, seeing his face — I was quarrelling with him! I always do when he won't give in to me — then I saw the bus. Oh, it was horrible, horrible! One minute it wasn't there, and then it was — big and red and bearing down on me as if it were three times the size of a normal bus! I'll never forget it as long as I live.'

'Don't! Don't cry — Sister will come in and scold me and she won't let me come and see you again. Don't!'

That had the effect of stilling the girl's wild crying. Barbara cautiously mopped the tears from that poor hurt face. Already they were stinging.

'You must try and forget about it,' Barbara told her. 'It's the only way to get well quickly.'

'But I want Damien to know how sorry I am for — for everything,' Margaret gasped. 'Go and tell him for me, will you? *Will* you?'

Her imperious manner was rather disconcerting. Barbara was nonplussed. In such instances the patient was given in to, if it was thought that the indulgence would help. She was certainly working herself up to a feverish state over it.

'I'm willing to do anything you want,' Barbara said, hoping that, in listening, Margaret would calm down, see reason and change her request. 'But would it do any good? I mean, if it's necessary to say that to him, wouldn't it be better coming from you yourself, when you're well enough to see him personally?'

The point of view recommended itself to Margaret for a moment or two. Then she shook her head again.

'No, no, I want him to know now. I'd write a letter if I could but — these wretched bandages on my hands — oh, what did I want to be such a fool for? Why didn't I wait until we got to the studios before I told him off? Oh, if only I could turn back the clock!'

Sister came in then with the R.S.O.

'What is wrong, Nurse?' she asked sharply, after one look at Margaret.

It was Margaret who answered. 'She won't do what I asked her to do for me, Sister. I only wanted her to go and take a message to my fiancé but she won't, she won't!'

'I will, if the patient really insists, Sister,' Barbara said quickly, but her voice was distressed. 'It was only that it was rather a personal message, but if you think I should, I don't mind trying, really I don't.'

'Will you tell him what I said?' Margaret insisted.

'All right, I will,' Barbara agreed, 'if Sister says so.'

'Now? This minute?'

'Well — ' Barbara hesitated, looking at Sister. It was all very well for Margaret Knowles to insist, but there was Sister of Men's Surgical to consult as well. It might not be convenient to go crashing into a private ward at any odd time.

The R.S.O. had his fingers on Margaret's pulse and looked round, nodding.

'Yes, Nurse shall go at once,' Sister said, quickly. She turned to Barbara and said, in a low voice, 'Tell Sister Rainer I sent you. It will be all right. Then come back here and tell the patient what Mr. Eldridge said. We must settle the patient as quickly as possible.'

Barbara hurried away, down the long

corridors and over the bridge to Men's Surgical, her mind in a turmoil. What would Adam Thorne say if he knew how Margaret was behaving? Or did he know already?

Sister Rainer was off duty and Staff was bothered by the latest mess her newest junior had got into. Over her shoulder she answered Barbara's request to see Damien Eldridge; distractedly: 'Yes, why not, if Sister Henty says it's important! I don't suppose he'll mind — the more the merrier!' And she returned to scolding the junior who was on the floor picking up the broken pieces of a tray load of mugs.

Barbara made herself scarce, closing the door behind her. The Staff Nurse was new to the job. It wasn't so long since Barbara herself had been the burden on the back of a very new S.R.N. and she didn't need to be told that the atmosphere was very electric indeed in there.

There was no sound of voices in

Damien's room, nor was the engaged tab on the door, so she knocked softly and went in.

The sight in that little room staggered her. There must have been at least a dozen people there. Several were bending over the bed, watching Damien Eldridge writing something on a long typewritten sheet. The others were standing around, silently waiting for the star to finish the job in hand. They all turned to see who had opened the door.

Barbara found herself the cynosure of all those eyes — an experience far more unnerving than that of walking on a ward first thing in the morning, when all the patients turned to look. That, too, had been unnerving at first, but not like this!

'Oh, I'm sorry, I didn't know — ' she stammered. 'I came with a message, but I'll come back later.'

Yet, as she said it, she knew that wouldn't do. If Margaret were still making a fuss, upsetting herself, then Sister would want her back with the star's answer, and how could she hope to get that at the moment?

Damien Eldridge recovered quickly. He had an eye for a pretty girl under any circumstances, and even the severe cap favoured by the Matron of the Hopwood General Hospital couldn't disguise the fact that here indeed was a very lovely young woman.

'I say, don't go away,' he called. 'Do come in — don't mind these chaps. They're not supposed to be here really but they would insist on coming to get these things signed. Do stay!'

'Yes, come along into the light and let's have a look at you,' the man holding the freshly signed document said.

'You don't understand,' Barbara said quietly, bracing herself. 'I have to see Mr. Eldridge alone. Sister on Women's Surgical sent me. It is urgent, I'm afraid. Perhaps your friends could go out for a few moments, Mr. Eldridge, while I deliver the message, and then they could come back? Do you mind?'

'A lovely voice, too!' one of the men said to Damien, taking no notice of the suggestion Barbara had so tactfully tried to make. 'Now look, old boy, wouldn't this solve everything? It's an idea — how about it now? Time's the essence, you know.'

Damien looked up at him. 'It *is* an idea,' he agreed. 'Come over by the bed, Nurse. You can deliver your message — these are all my friends as well as my colleagues. I have no secrets from them!'

Barbara stood there appalled. How on earth could she tell him, in front of all those people, that Margaret wanted him to know that she was sorry for making that scene in the car, which she believed had been the cause of the accident?

4

One of the women in the party — brisk and efficient and terribly smart — broke in.

'Let's behave like perfect little angels,' she said, coolly, 'and do as the nurse suggests and go out and leave those two together. Come on, boys!'

She nodded at them, exchanging a meaning look all round and, to Barbara's surprise and relief, they all agreed. They took their leave assuring Damien they'd be back in ten minutes' time.

As the last one closed the door Damien Eldridge grinned widely and engagingly at her.

'I'm not really supposed to have all that lot in at once, anyway! Sister's off duty, otherwise it could never have happened. That poor Staff Nurse is so distracted she probably never even saw them come sneaking in.'

'I wondered how it had come about,' Barbara confessed, uneasily.

The room made her distinctly uncomfortable. Everywhere possible small tables had been put, to take the masses of flowers, the signed photographs of film personalities in expensive frames, the portable television set, the radio, a desk over-spilling with papers, and chairs for his visitors.

There were three chairs. Barbara wondered what Sister would say if she ever found out about this impromptu party he appeared to have been having. Someone had brought in a bottle of sherry and some glasses apparently; she distinctly remembered seeing most of the people standing about holding a filled glass, just as if it were a cocktail party, and not a private ward off the surgical wing of a hospital!

She was so uncomfortable in this alien atmosphere that she was at a loss to know how to begin.

'What was it you had to tell me?' he

prompted her, gently, his eyes never leaving her face.

'Honestly, I don't know how to tell you,' she confessed. 'Sister detailed me to come along to you at once and give you what the patient said was a message, because, well, Miss Knowles was working herself up and she's too ill to be allowed to do that.'

His smile faded. 'You're speaking of Margaret — my fiancée?' he said, as if making quite certain there was no mistake. 'What was the message?'

'That's just it!' Barbara replied, helplessly. 'Sister didn't know, but, it wasn't really a message so much as a — well, it's very embarrassing. She should have told you herself only that wasn't possible. You see, before Sister came into the room, your fiancée was talking to me, and getting rather worked up about the accident.'

'I see.' He looked down at his beautifully manicured hands. 'She was saying whose fault she thought it was, no doubt?'

He sounded weary, rather than upset. As if this were something he didn't want to hear, because he knew it already.

'She says it was her fault and she's so sorry about it now and wants you to know,' Barbara said, firmly.

He looked surprised at that. 'She said that, did she? She didn't, by any chance, admit that we'd been quarrelling at the time?'

'Yes, she said that, too. She was also very upset about how the sight of the bus coming at her still haunts her, particularly at night.'

'Yes, me too,' he said, quietly. 'It will live with me for the rest of my life, but unlike Margaret, I have the capacity for putting things behind me. Nothing I can do or say will undo that accident so — I refuse to let it ruin my life or the things I had set out to do.'

It sounded harsh but Barbara realised that he was half talking to himself.

'So you see, Mr. Eldridge, why I had to say this to you privately and not in front of your friends,' she added, desperately.

He smiled kindly at her and patted her hand.

'Not to worry,' he asured her. 'I understand. Was there anything else?'

Barbara nodded. 'Only that she wants a message to go back to her. To reassure her.'

'Oh, yes,' he said, softly, a wry smile touching his lips. 'Margaret would, of course, want that. I'll write a note for her. How's that?'

'Oh, no, not another note, please! I've already had to read one personal note aloud to her,' Barbara said, flushing. 'Well, it was from a friend.' She floundered badly. Perhaps Damien, having stolen Margaret from some other man, might be the jealous type who wouldn't want to know that the same thing was being done to him.

Damien, however, was made of different stuff. The thing that concerned him was why Margaret had had to have the note read to her. 'Is it her eyes?' he asked quickly.

'No. No, it's her hands — they're bandaged, and she can't use them to open a letter.'

'Then it will have to be a verbal message. Tell her, if you will, that I send her all my love and look forward to seeing her soon. Oh, and assure her that I understand about the accident. Tell her not to worry. I know we were arguing at the time, but I understand that the bus driver was also at fault so . . . make her see I mean that. She isn't to worry.'

'I'll do all that, sir,' Barbara said, preparing to go.

'What are you calling me 'sir' for?' he asked, smiling lop-sidedly. 'Everyone calls me Damien, from the producer down to the crossing-sweeper at the studio gates. Why do you have to be so terribly up-stage?'

'Oh, it wasn't meant for that, I assure you. It's just the way we — '

'Only teasing,' he chuckled. 'But call

me Damien. Everyone does. What's your name?'

'Barbara Caley. But I really must go now.'

'Do something for me, will you? When you have a minute, if you're not too busy that is, drop in and let me know how Margaret took my message. I'd like to know she's settled. Tell her, Get-well-soon.'

She nodded and fled.

There was no sign of any of his friends outside. They had either had the wit to make themselves scarce or they had been discovered by Sister and sent away.

Sue was immensely intrigued to hear all about it that evening. 'Why didn't you go back and see him, just as he asked, you chump!' she exploded. 'I would have done!'

'I did think about it. Margaret Knowles wanted me to in the first place, but I hardly think that meant I was to go back again. She's rather possessive about him, I think. She might have thought I wanted to get friendly with him behind her back.'

'Well, how about getting me in to see him?' Sue demanded.

'Nothing doing!' Barbara said, laughing.

'All right,' the incorrigible Sue went on, 'what was all that about you solving their problem? Sounds as if they had something in mind for you. Don't you want to find out what it was about?'

'I think those friends of his had been sipping sherry too early in the day and that they wanted to have a bit of fun with the first young nurse who happened to come into the room and I happened to be it. No thanks, I don't think I'll venture into the middle of one of Damien Eldridge's parties again.'

'I believe you're stuck on him!' Sue gurgled. 'Yes, you are. You're blushing!'

'I might be if he weren't engaged already to that girl. He's a very nice person, not at all like what one expects a film star to be like. I thought he'd only be interested in hearing someone say that they'd seen all his pictures and of how wonderful they thought he was. But he isn't like that, not really. He's a very real person.'

'Then go along and see him again. He's asked you to!'

'No, I'm sure he didn't really mean it,' Barbara insisted and, as far as she was concerned, the matter was closed.

But it wasn't too easy to put the thought of him from her mind, because of the contact with Margaret. Although Barbara didn't go to Margaret's home to collect some clothes for her, as she had asked, Barbara did tell Sister that the patient was pining for some pretty things.

They decided to ask Margaret's aunt to bring some on her next visit. The old lady did so with misgivings but, even when Margaret had been dressed up in a gorgeous bed-jacket trimmed with white fur, to receive her visitors, she had no word of thanks for Barbara's efforts. She was imperious in her demands for service and other people's time, and it never occurred to her to say thank you.

And the subject of Damien nagged at her so much that she fell into the habit of sending Barbara over to him with messages and demanding answers.

Damien was very much embarrassed about it.

'Oh, I say, I'm sorry she's giving you all this trouble, really I am,' he told Barbara. 'Why don't you tell her you're too busy to be at her beck and call?'

'I don't mind. I'd do anything to help a patient,' Barbara protested. 'Sister knows, and she agrees that we must do anything we can to put Miss Knowles' mind at rest and get her well again. She's your fiancée — you should be glad that everyone's so anxious to do what they can for her.'

He was resting on his bed, after being up for a little while and today, Barbara noticed, he looked rather over-tired. She wondered if all those friends of his had sneaked in again and worried him.

'You don't understand, Barbara.

76

You're so sweet and uncomplicated,' he said, at last. 'I was wrong all along the line, right from the time I first met Margaret. It's almost a judgment on me, I suppose. It's not actually true what they say — I didn't just set out to take her from that other fellow. She went half way to meet me and at first she kept it from me that there was anyone else in her life. Oh, I'm not trying to excuse myself for what I did, but now I feel such a heel because I don't want to go on being engaged to her.'

He looked at Barbara then, and she saw how distressed he was.

'You think I'm pretty hard, don't you, to say this now, but it's true. What we were quarrelling about in the car that day was the same subject. I was goaded to tell her that I couldn't go on. I should, of course, have waited till we arrived, not worried her while she was driving, but there it is. I didn't want her any more then, and the situation hasn't altered. But what am I to do?'

'Are you sure you feel like that, really?' she whispered. 'But that's terrible! She's just clinging to the thought of you. If she got to hear you felt like that, she'd just give up.'

'I know that only too well,' he agreed, soberly. 'And I've no intention of letting her get to know, before she's fully recovered.'

'Why did you tell me, then?'

'I feel I know you, Barbara. Just through these odd little visits of yours, running messages for Margaret. I feel that you're one of the few people I can thoroughly trust. I wish I had met you first,' he said, putting his hand on hers. She coloured, her heart bumping unevenly. She was well aware that she, too, wished the same thing. But it couldn't be. He was Margaret's and it was doubly incumbent on him to stay Margaret's, having taken her from someone else and broken up that someone else's life.

'I have to go back now,' she said, getting up. 'What shall I tell her today?'

'Just how is she?' he asked her. 'Come on, tell me the truth, as far as you know it. Unless you've been forbidden to, of course.'

'You know the rules,' she told him, evenly. 'We're not allowed to discuss one patient with another.'

'Who will tell me about her, then? Everyone else shies away from the subject, as if the outcome will be too horrible to contemplate.'

'She's very ill and she isn't giving herself a chance,' Barbara admitted, 'because she keeps getting worked up when she doesn't get her own way.'

'That's my Margaret!' he said, softly.

'But I think there's a very good chance that she'll be about again, in time.'

'That sounds grim.'

'Oh, for goodness' sake, don't hold me to it! You wanted some idea, and I don't know too much about it myself. I'm not even on her ward. That's just the impression I get, and I thought it might help you to know.'

'Don't worry, Barbara, I won't let anyone know you told me — but this is between ourselves. Barbara, do I really have to stick by her, stay engaged to her, regardless of what happens?'

She tried to pull her hand away, blushing furiously. There was no doubt what he was getting at.

'I think you've answered your own question,' she said. 'Of course you do! This isn't the time to make any changes, no matter what you were feeling like at the time of the accident. And I believe you know that perfectly well.'

'Well, I can hardly say what I intend to say, after that outburst, can I?' He managed to smile at her but it was plain he didn't feel like smiling. 'But if Margaret comes through this all right, then I'm going to break it off. Don't you forget that — and you know why I want to break it off with her, don't you?'

'Please don't. I wish you wouldn't. My feeling is that you're the only man in the world for her and she must have been the one for you, too, or you wouldn't have been keen enough on her to — well, do what you did!'

'I suppose I deserved that, Barbara, but it isn't true. I was dazzled, yes, but I've discovered since that it wasn't love.'

'It might be the same again, with some other girl,' she thrust at him. She had to say something sharp so that there would be no likelihood of his guessing how she felt. There was nothing in the world she would have liked more than to be the one girl in his life. She had never met anyone like him before, and she loved his gentle way with her. It would be so easy to let him go on thinking that she would wait for him until he got free from Margaret Knowles.

But it wasn't in her to do that.

'Before you go there's something else I want to say to you,' Damien said, on a new note. 'Do you remember what my friends were saying that first time you came into this room? They said it might be the answer to our problems. Remember? Or weren't you listening to what they were saying to me?'

'Yes, I do remember. But at the time I thought it might be some sort of joke.'

'It wasn't a joke, I assure you. When I come out of here I've got to find a small-part actress as near Margaret's build and colouring as possible, for a screen test — or else we shall have to hold up production even longer. We shall have lost quite enough money as it is. We can't afford to lose any more by waiting for Margaret.'

'She's depending on that, too,' Barbara said, in a low voice. 'She tells me every day about that part you're going to arrange for her.'

He shook his head impatiently.

'Frankly, I don't think she would have passed the test before the accident, and she's no actress, but I had to agree. Ours is a small company and a lot of her aunt's money's in it as well as her own. Be that as it may, I can't wait any longer. My friends thought you'd fill the bill very well. Have you ever thought of going into pictures?'

5

Barbara was so surprised she could hardly speak.

'I mean it,' Damien said, very seriously.

'How can you mean it?' she retorted, when she got her breath back. 'You don't know if I'd photograph well and you certainly don't know whether I can act. Besides — '

'Wait! Before you say any more let me say this. That in the film business one gets a sort of instinct about people. Sometimes one can be wrong, but usually not. I should say that you'd be definitely photogenic.'

'But that only means that I'd come up all right on the screen, doesn't it? Isn't it a fact that one still has to have some experience of acting? Well, let's be reasonable — I've never done such a thing in my life!'

'You might find you had a natural flair for it but, for a small part like this, you'd have to be very wooden indeed to be a flop. You just have to do as you're told and be natural.'

'Then why do you think Margaret Knowles would have been no good at it?' Barbara said, swiftly, quickly bringing the subject back to his fiancée. It was getting dangerously out of hand, she felt. This nonsense must be stopped.

If she was quick to turn the subject he was even quicker with his retort.

'In the first place, Margaret never did as she was told in her life, and she's never likely too!' he said.

They stared at each other. He seemed doomed to say things about Margaret which would bring forth Barbara's disapproval.

'Well, my dear, you did ask me,' he said, quietly. 'It also happens that she isn't particularly photogenic but she is insisting on a screen test. She wants to be in pictures, and, although she's settled for a small part, it's only to be a sort of thin edge of the wedge. In her heart she sees herself as a great actress and we all know that's wishful thinking of the highest. It promised to be awkward enough handling her over this before the accident; now it looks like being well-nigh impossible.'

'You're not going to make it any easier asking someone else to do the job meantime,' Barbara objected. 'If you don't mind my saying so, I think it's a mad idea to think of someone like me for the job considering that I've never set foot in a film studio, let alone tried even the most amateur dramatics.'

'I wanted you,' Damien said, softly. 'Perhaps I didn't go about it in the right way. Think about it, will you? Don't turn down the idea straight away. Sleep on it, and let me know fairly soon. I really mean it, and it is important to me — to my friends, too — in a way that you'd perhaps find difficult to understand.'

She got up, shaking her head again.

'There isn't any point in thinking any more about it. I can't do it. There's another reason.'

'Going to tell me what it is or shouldn't I ask?' he said, grimacing a little.

'Well, it's this. I am training to be a nurse. I want to finish my training. I can't break off to do anything else. And, to be honest, I don't think I'd want to.'

He looked really surprised at that but he recovered himself quickly and, taking her hand again, squeezed it and said persuasively, 'I can't help feeling that if you got a glimpse of the film world you might think again. So — please don't say a definite no. Not just yet. Wait till I'm about again and can show you around . . . and see a picture being made. I think you might change your mind.'

He was being too persuasive. She left him before he could say any more.

Sue was tremendously impressed when she heard about it. They were walking sedately side by side into the town that evening, and Sue came to a full stop in astonishment.

'What! He offered you a screen test? Oh, Bar, you lucky, lucky thing!'

'Well, don't shout. Everybody's looking,' Barbara pointed out, taking her friend's arm and hurrying her on. 'Besides, it doesn't really mean a thing.'

'Of course it does! Oh, if only I'd been the one!'

'What would you have done in my place?' Barbara asked, curiously.

'Well, I'd have snapped up the offer before he had time to change his mind! You'd better buck up and say yes, anyway, because he's going home soon.'

'I can't take such an offer, Sue, even if I wanted to. How could I?'

'In your holiday! How long have you got due to you?'

'A couple of weeks. Oh, but I couldn't. It wouldn't be right. Supposing by sheer bad luck I got through and had to take that part? It would be like stabbing Margaret Knowles in the back.'

'Of course it wouldn't. She's so rich she doesn't need the money. She just fancies herself as a screen actress, and you said yourself that Damien Eldridge doesn't think much of her talent. But he thinks he's spotted a winner in you.'

'But that was in confidence, Sue. If you say it out loud like that anyone might hear.'

'What, in the crowded High Street? Don't be silly!' Sue scoffed. 'Now listen, someone's got to talk some sense into your head — ' she began, but she was interrupted by a man's voice calling from behind.

They both turned to find the Casualty Officer right on their heels.

'Nurse Caley, could I have a word with you?' he said, formally.

'Yes, of course,' Barbara told him at once.

'I'm going, anyway,' Sue said, hastily. 'We were only just walking to the bus station together. See you later, Bar.'

She set off at a smart pace leaving Barbara to face Adam Thorne.

He looked rather put out. 'I don't want to keep you,' he said. 'I just wanted to ask you how Miss Knowles seemed today? I haven't been up.'

'It's all right, Mr. Thorne. I was only going for a walk to the bus stop with Nurse Gardner. Miss Knowles,' she went on, answering his enquiry, 'doesn't seem any worse but she doesn't get any better, either. She's worrying about all the things she wanted to do when the accident happened. And now she's just forced to lie in bed and wait.'

'Such as having a screen test?' he asked, with a grim look. 'And you, too? Have you been invited to have a test as well? I heard what your friend said. Is it true?'

'Yes, it is, but I refused the offer,' Barbara said, quietly.

'Why?'

'I don't think it would answer!' she said, shortly.

He suggested they might walk along and he fell into step beside her.

'I see. I thought perhaps you had

decided to — well, I suppose no one can blame you if you said yes to such an offer. Most young women would, to judge by your friend's excitement.'

'Sue's all right,' Barbara said, quickly. 'Only she doesn't understand. She's never really met Mr. Eldridge and she doesn't know Miss Knowles.'

'And you think you do?' But he was smiling a little as he said it.

'I spend a little time with her every day now,' Barbara pointed out.

'Yes, I know that, and I never get a chance to thank you properly. I want to thank you now, anyway, and if I spoke rather sharply to you a few moments ago it was only because I'm so anxious about Miss Knowles.'

They had reached the bridge and he stopped, staring unseeingly at a long boat with a string of barges behind it as it appeared underneath them.

'Miss Knowles,' he said, almost as if speaking to himself, 'is to have an operation soon. I believe that if we can all make her feel that everything is to be

91

just as she wishes it, including that ill-fated screen test, she will come through all right.'

'You don't have to worry,' Barbara said, impulsively.

'I tell her she'll be all right, every day, and I do my best with her messages to Mr. Eldridge.'

She had been going to say — but bit the words back just in time — that she usually dressed up his return messages to make them sound more enthusiastic. That would never do, she remembered, if it were true that Adam Thorne still cared for Margaret Knowles.

'Don't fill her with too much hope,' he said, with sharp anxiety giving an edge to his voice. 'It will be a long time before she gets back to the sort of life she was living — to any brisk activity, in fact!'

'It isn't that which really worries me,' Barbara confessed.

'Then what is it?'

'My friend just reminded me that Mr. Eldridge was to be allowed to go home soon. What will happen then?'

'That will be better for Miss Knowles, I imagine!' he said. 'Eldridge will be able to visit her in person. He could go now, if he liked. Does he realise that he can be taken up in a chair? There's a lift at that end. What's to stop him?'

Barbara knew perfectly well what was to stop Damien from visiting Margaret. He liked Barbara to take the messages and stop and talk to him. He shrank from seeing Margaret's face, or getting involved in one of her emotional scenes. But it was more than she dared do to say so.

'He looked rather tired when I visited him, I thought,' she did venture to suggest. 'Perhaps it's a little too much for him just yet.'

Adam Thorne grunted. 'Well, we can't stay here talking. Look here, did you really mean it when you said you weren't bound for anywhere in particular? Well, why don't we go and get a meal somewhere? There was something else I wanted to discuss with you. How about it?'

'I'd like to very much,' Barbara said. Her heart ached for him nowadays. He was taking all this so hard. If there was only something that she could find to say, to help him, it would be well worth sitting through a meal somewhere, instead of a sandwich and taking the brisk walk she had been thinking of.

But, in the end, she enjoyed the meal very much and she also enjoyed his company. He took her to one of the family hotels at the end of the town where the big shops were. He was apparently well known and got excellent service. The food was good, too. Barbara sat back and felt relaxed for the first time for days.

'You're tired out,' he said, suddenly. 'Are you finding Casualty too much for you?'

'Oh, no, not at all,' she said, quickly. 'Well, not really, but of course it is more tiring than the wards. I suppose it's the uncertainty of it all. You never know what's coming next!'

'And do you, on the wards?' he smiled.

'Well, no, not all the time, but there is a set routine of work and somehow it seems more peaceful.'

'Peaceful!' He seemed surprised. 'Is that what you want . . . to be peaceful? You wouldn't get that kind of existence if you went and had a screen test, you know. I believe it's a very hectic life.'

'But you forget — I don't want that kind of life. I told Mr. Eldridge so.'

A shadow crossed Adam Thorne's face at the mention of the man who had taken away his fiancée.

'What did he have to say to that?' he asked.

'I don't think he really believed me.'

'And Miss Knowles doesn't really believe you, either, when you come back with fond messages from him,' Adam Thorne said, quietly.

It staggered her. It was a minute or two before she could speak and, when she did, it was barely a whisper.

'Did she tell you so?'

He nodded. 'Not today. Yesterday. I found her in one of those tense moods of hers. It's very disheartening. We get her cheered up and then she finds something else to fret about.'

'But what else can I do?' Barbara cried.

'I don't know. I wish I did,' Adam Thorne confessed. 'I've thought about it until I'm confused. I can't begin to see the thing clearly. I blame myself for ever having bothered you to take those gifts up to her for me.' His face crumpled into one of those rare sweet smiles of his.

'You had asked me some time before, if you could do anything for me, I remember, and you had looked so touchingly young and kind. I thought of you as just the right person for poor Margaret to set eyes on.'

That filled her with confusion. She had been so sure that he had just asked her because she happened to be the one who was nearest. She had forgotten that she had offered to help him earlier on. He must have looked infinitely weary and harassed at the time. He often did and it made her feel so helpless, as if it were her personal responsibility. At that moment she wished for nothing more than to be able to lose that odd sensation when she looked at him.

Why should she feel like that about him? He wasn't her business. He was just the Casualty Officer, for whom she occasionally worked, as did many other young nurses. Why should she worry over him? He was years older than herself and, presumably, well able to take care of himself, without her worrying about him.

But is wasn't as easy as that. He would continue to have that effect on her, she was only too well aware, and she could do little about it.

'And I was right, you see,' he went on. 'Margaret was so pleased with you. She thanked me for picking someone like you, and not — well, not one of the more practical and older nurses.'

Margaret had said 'old battle-axes' but that, of course, was hardly the remark to pass on to a student nurse.

'Doesn't she like me any more?' Barbara faltered.

'This is very difficult. How can I put it? You do all the things she asks you but somehow she has heard that you stay and talk to Eldridge. I don't know how these things get about, but there it is. Now she's fretting because she thinks she'll lose Eldridge to you.'

She could see only too well that he didn't like having to say that to her. There was nothing she could say, either. The damage was done.

'Is it true?' he pursued. 'But you knew he was engaged to her from the start.'

She drew a deep breath.

'Yes, I know that, and I haven't done or said anything that would let him think I liked him specially. I do — but that's beside the point. The whole thing is, Mr. Thorne, he doesn't want Margaret any more. Oh, don't look like that! He isn't going to give her up or even let her know he feels like that now, because she's so ill. He told me he wouldn't.'

'He discussed his feelings for her, with you?'

'Well, I was the one sent to and fro with their personal messages,' she protested, with heightened colour. 'It was inevitable that I should be dragged into it, I suppose.'

'Yes. I'm very sorry indeed that I started it.'

'Please don't be. I think it would have been the same, whoever was close to Miss Knowles. You see, you may not know this, but Mr. Eldridge told me that he was trying to break their engagement off, the day of the accident. That's what they were arguing about in the car, at the time.' She couldn't bring herself to use the word 'quarrelling'. It seemed so dreadful for two people engaged to be married, acting like that so often that they lost the sense of where they were, and continued their disagreement in a car among traffic.

He shot his head up. That was news to him.

'Are you sure? Oh, I know they were having a disagreement in the car — Margaret told me. But she didn't disclose what it was about. I thought it was about this part in the film.'

'It was, indirectly. He doesn't feel she's got it in her to do it. And he doesn't want to marry her. But he's promised me he won't let her know until — '

'Yes, Nurse Caley — until when? That is the question, isn't it?' He was angry again now. 'And how does that young man think he's going to keep such a thing from her? His messages lack warmth and he doesn't come in person to see her now that he is able to!'

'But surely, Mr. Thorne, she must know how he feels? She must remember the scene in the car that day. She hasn't lost her memory! Or does she think his feelings have changed because she was so badly injured?'

'Pity?' he murmured, frowning doubtfully. 'I don't know. I just don't know.'

'What do you want me to do?' Barbara asked him, genuine anxiety creasing her face.

'Haven't you got a man-friend of your own?' he asked, thinking. 'It occurred to me that you might talk to Margaret about him: make her see it was him you were thinking of all the time, and not the man she cares for.'

She looked searchingly at him. It struck her then that he wasn't in love with Margaret Knowles, so much as terribly concerned for her physical welfare, and angry that this trick of fate should undermine all the hospital was trying to do for her. Barbara didn't understand it at all.

'I can't help you there. There isn't any one special in my life. I can invent one if you like but I doubt if she would believe me.'

'No, I wouldn't want you to do that,'

Adam Thorne said, quickly. 'I've asked you to do more than enough. I'm not asking you to lie for me. No, all I hope you'll be able to do is to persuade Eldridge to go in person and see her before he is discharged. Surely that wouldn't be too difficult?'

Barbara promised to do what she could, but she hadn't much hope. She didn't quite understand the Casualty Officer's attitude. What did he expect? Half the nurses in the hospital were a little in love with Damien. He did that to young women, especially those who happened to be unattached.

The next time she saw Damien, however, she did try to persuade him.

He was walking with a stick now, the injured leg in plaster with a caliper on it. He seemed much less fatigued than on that other occasion.

He stood there, in a gorgeous silk dressing-gown, a silk scarf tucked in at the throat, looking as well-groomed and suave and charming as he had so many times on the screen. She hadn't realised that he was such a slight man, and he seemed less tall, too, than she had imagined. Clever camera shots had given the impression of slender height, but he wasn't as tall as Adam Thorne. Nor as strong-looking, she found herself adding, mentally.

'You really mean, Barbara, that you want me to go up there and tell her I love her, face to face with her? She'd never believe me!'

'You're an actor! Make her believe you!' she flared.

'But why? Why? I shall be stuck with her for ever. You don't know Margaret Knowles. If I didn't want her any more when she was fit and well, I certainly shrink from the thought of her playing up to being an invalid. She'd give me hell! And I believe you know it! You must have some idea what she's really like! Look at the way she uses you, and you're not the only one! No, I'm sorry, Barbara, I just couldn't do it.'

'Even though it might make her so ill and weak with fretting that she won't have the strength to stand up to the operation and what is to come after that!'

He moved his shoulders irritably.

'I don't believe it depends on me to that extent! No one else has said so.'

'Mr. Thorne has, and so has Sister Henty and Sister Rainer,' Barbara pointed out.

'And you've been sent along to try and persuade me. Why? Because they think that that baby-face and those appealing blue eyes will do the trick? Perhaps they're right. You *are* appealing, Barbara. In fact, I find it devilish hard to resist you. But unless I do I shall be losing you. You know that, don't you? You know how much I — '

'Please don't say it,' she said, sharply.

'Say what?' He pretended to be surprised, just to tease her. 'What did you think I was going to say?'

'I think you were going to say all the things that male patients often say to their nurses. It's a sort of aftermath of the time spent in hospital. We're used to it. When the patients get outside into their own world again they often wonder why on earth they got worked up about this or that nurse. Probably they're quite relieved that the nurses in question weren't unduly impressed.'

'You've got all the answers, haven't you?' he said, at last. 'You're writing me off as just another infatuated male gone silly over a pretty young nurse. Well, it isn't like that, and you'll see, later on. Meantime, I suppose I'd better have another think about seeing Margaret before I leave the hospital. You see how much I like to please you!' he said, taking her chin in his hand. 'You've the most delightful chin I've ever seen on a woman.'

She thought, for one moment of panic, that he was going to try to kiss her. She ducked away.

'I don't want you to go and see Miss Knowles just to please me, but to please *her!*' she protested.

'Even the motive has got to be right, eh? You are a little slave-driver,

Barbara,' but he was laughing softly and, as she left him and sped along the corridors, back to Casualty, she really felt, with a lightened heart, that she had achieved her object and that, for whatever reason, he would go and see Margaret, and try to convince her that everything was still the same between them.

* * *

Barbara and Sue had two days off. They had planned to go and stay with some relatives of Sue's, on a farm. She had looked forward to it so much. Sue's uncle — who had been on the ward near Damien's door — enjoyed that rare thing, a week-end in the heart of a big family.

Casualty seemed a long, long way away, but once Barbara's heart turned over, as she caught sight of a tall, rangy figure striding across the fields with one of Sue's male cousins. A figure in rough tweeds, leather gaiters, a turned down old felt and a gun under one arm.

For a moment she had thought it was Adam Thorne. A ridiculous thought, when she recognised a neighbouring farmer. It was just the height and that rather loping walk that caught her off guard.

Bewildered, she wondered why she couldn't forget him now she was so far away from the hospital. But she couldn't. She remembered Adam Thorne in a thousand ways; smiling whimsically at her, or angry with her; looking worried about Margaret, or deeply tender over an injured child. His face and his voice seemed to haunt her, and it bothered her. In comparison, she thought of Damien quite rarely, but then Damien hadn't worried her nor made her feel that urgent sense of responsibility that Adam Thorne did.

At last that wonderful week-end came to an end and she and Sue returned to duty, both very much refreshed from that stretch of hours in pure country air, far away from the sound of ambulance bells and the sight of injured humanity.

The first thing that greeted Barbara when she went back to Casualty was the sight of Adam Thorne striding in, looking sharply from right to left until he located her.

'You promised me you'd tackle Eldridge about seeing Miss Knowles,' he began. 'Didn't you?'

'Yes! Yes, I did, Mr. Thorne. And he promised — well, half-promised — to go up and see her before he left. Didn't he do that?'

'He left without a word to her,' Adam Thorne said, his face extremely grim.

'I can't believe it! He made a joke of it and said he supposed he would have to go, even though he knew it wouldn't be very sensible.'

'What did he mean by that, Nurse?'

'I took it that he meant that she would know he was only doing it because she was ill. She knew he didn't want to and nothing he could do or say would alter that.'

'I see. Well, he didn't go to see her. He left without a word as I've said — and she found out somehow that he'd been discharged a day earlier than she had expected. It was a shock. A great shock.'

'Oh, dear! Has it — put her back?' Barbara faltered.

'Put her back!' he echoed. '*She collapsed!*'

6

The news staggered Barbara.

'Oh, how dreadful, Mr. Thorne!' she exclaimed.

'What is going to happen?'

'It's certain that she can't be operated on until she has quietened down again,' he said briefly. 'It isn't a thing one can cure with drugs. And the aggravating part of it is that it need not have happened. She just wants to know that she's secure — that the one person in the world who means something to her is there, beside her. It doesn't seem a lot to ask, does it? Or does it, Nurse?'

She was puzzled. 'What do you mean by that, Mr. Thorne? I don't understand!'

'I think you know perfectly well what I mean, Nurse. You like Eldridge and you've made him like you! You admitted as much to me not so many hours ago, didn't you?'

'That isn't fair!' she was moved to exclaim. 'I certainly said I liked him, but you're suggesting that I've deliberately taken him away from the patient. That just isn't true!'

'I should need proof of that,' he said quietly.

'How can I prove any such thing to you? I can't force him to visit the patient, or to stay in love with her. I told you what he said — they were finished at the time of the accident. I keep saying so.'

'Very well. You don't leave me any alternative. I want that young man here, in this hospital, at the patient's bed-side, and I want you to get him!'

'But how *can* I?' she cried. 'I can't make him do anything he doesn't want to — and quite obviously he hadn't any intention of visiting her, before he left the hospital. If you feel so strongly about it, Mr. Thorne, why don't you order him to come, yourself?'

'What do you mean, Nurse — 'if I feel so strongly about it'?'

There was an edge to his voice. She knew she had gone too far, but she couldn't help it.

She considered his manner intolerable. There would have been some justification to it, if she had set out to get Damien Eldridge, to make him notice her and fall for her. But that had been the last thing she had tried to do. He himself had made all the running, while she had done her best to keep him at bay.

So she said, spiritedly, 'I don't mean to be rude, Mr. Thorne, but frankly it really isn't my responsibility. Don't you think you should be the one to arrange it? You knew Miss Knowles before. I hadn't even met her previous to that day when you asked me to go up to her with your gifts! I've done my best, but it's hardly my fault if her engagement is a failure.'

'I see,' he said, but he was quieter now. 'Very well, then, I'll tell you why I feel so strongly about all this. Miss Knowles and I happen to be — er — very old friends. Her aunt and my family have known each other since we were children. I'm sure you will agree that it isn't unusual to feel strongly about a person in those circumstances?'

She flushed a little. He had a good argument there, and knocked sideways her previous feeling that he was taking a very odd stand, as the jilted lover, trying to bring back the new lover. But, of course, she couldn't voice those thoughts of hers.

'I might add,' he put in for good measure, 'that another reason why I'm asking you to be the one to get Eldridge here is that you know him personally, and I don't!' and with that shattering rejoinder, he walked off.

The perfect exit, she thought, rather resentfully, watching him stride away. There was something in the set of his shoulders that infuriated her. This was the man she had felt so responsible for, the man who tore at her heart because he looked so unhappy about Margaret Knowles!

What a fool she had been to care that much about him, Barbara told herself angrily. It was quite clear that he could very well take care of himself, and he knew how to get his own way, too, without bothering to exercise any charm over it.

Her anger against Adam Thorne was as much out of proportion as her previous pity and anxiety had been.

She didn't understand it, nor did she particularly care for it. But she couldn't forgive his high-handedness. There was no question of suggesting how she should go about getting Damien Eldridge to come here — she had just been ordered to get him, somehow, soon. Very well, she told herself, she would do just that!

But it wasn't going to be easy. At the time of the accident he had had no fixed address, but had been staying with friends since he had returned from Hollywood. The only place she knew of was the film studios, and that was where she made her first effort to contact Damien.

It took up a great deal of her free time, and in the end was very little immediate help. They finally told her that Damien had gone to the coast for a few days to recuperate, and he had left no note of where he was, because he hadn't wished to be disturbed. But she did discover from them that when he returned Damien would be staying with the producer and his wife at their flat in Maplefield.

That was something, even if it was the best that Barbara could manage. Damien had well and truly slipped away out of reach. He had meant what he said, that was clear — he had already grown tired of Margaret and her ways before the accident, and nothing on earth would make him change now.

This ruthlessness in Damien's make-up surprised Barbara. He had seemed such a nice young man, and to her the least he could have done was to have strung along with Margaret while she was so ill, and taken up any differences they may have had, when the patient was well enough. That, to Barbara, the nurse, was the only right and proper thing to do.

She fought with her own feelings over this, and tried to look at the thing in all its aspects. Margaret, of course, was very selfish. In all fairness to Damien, Barbara had to admit that Margaret didn't endear herself to anyone. Her moods were a great trial. Her wilfulness had already retarded her recovery in hospital — Barbara had heard two Staff Nurses discussing it only that morning. Everything had to be as Margaret wanted it, and her inflexibility of character tried the nursing staff to the last degree.

Still, she told herself, biting her lip in vexation, what if Damien, having got free of Margaret, should interest himself in Barbara herself, and something happened to Barbara? What would Damien do then — cut clear again at the first opportunity? It was a disturbing thought.

Barbara sighed, and went up to see if she could have a word with Margaret. It was almost the end of the day. She found Margaret's aunt sitting by her.

The old lady — very much like Margaret in features but possessing a sweetness that was missing in her niece's face — sat stiffly by the bed. Margaret tossed and turned, fretfully muttering a name. As she drew closer, Barbara knew that it was Damien that Margaret was asking for.

'Don't get up, Miss Whinfield,' Barbara whispered to the old lady. 'I just wanted to say hallo to her. I usually try to see her for a few minutes every day.'

The old lady nodded, and looked at her niece.

Margaret had caught the whispered remark and said resentfully, 'Not true. You haven't been to see me for days!'

'I've had a couple of days off. I went away with a friend.'

Margaret twisted her head sharply to look up at Barbara.

'You've been away with Damien!' she flared.

'Margaret, dear,' her aunt protested, scandalised.

'What a thing to say to your nurse!'

'She isn't my nurse — she's been getting friendly with him when I sent her to him with messages,' Margaret said. She said it dully, as if it were such a stale truth with her that she had long ago accepted it.

'I've been away with another nurse, a great friend of mine,' Barbara said quietly. 'And Mr. Eldridge is staying with friends on the coast, and he'll be coming back to visit you as soon as he can get about without tiring.'

It seemed the best thing to say, but Margaret didn't believe her. She began to cry again. Her injured face creased with anguish, and her aunt began to be upset.

'I shall have to call Sister,' Barbara warned. 'You have no right to get upset

118

like this. Everyone loves you and they are all waiting to see you again, longing to have you back. And you could be back much sooner, if you'd only be sensible and let everyone help you.'

'That's right, blame it on to me,' Margaret said childishly, but she did stop crying. Whether because Barbara's words had had any effect on her or whether the tears scorched her face too much for endurance, it was hard to say.

Nonetheless, when Barbara left Margaret's room, she was certainly more quiet, but her aunt was upset.

Barbara took Miss Whinfield to a waiting-room and got her a cup of tea, and sat with her while she drank it.

'Have you far to go home?' she asked gently.

'No. It's all right, Nurse. Mr. Thorne is driving me home in his car. He's very kind to me. I wish — '

'Yes?' Barbara asked gently.

'Perhaps I shouldn't say this. You probably don't know about it. Anyway, it's hardly your business. But it is nice to talk to someone and you have an inviting manner, my dear. You draw people out,' she sighed. 'I'm tempted to tell you about it.'

'Then why don't you? I know about Mr. Thorne having been engaged to your niece, you know. In confidence, everyone knows, and we're all so sorry about it.'

'Oh, then that's all right — I can talk about it! You see, I've never really understood what went wrong. I should dearly have loved him for a nephew-in-law. He's such a nice person. But there it was — something did go wrong, and before I knew what had happened, Margaret was all over this dreadful young actor of hers. I can't help it — I know everyone idolises him, but I think he's a dreadful young man!'

'Who do you mean, Miss Whinfield?' Barbara asked, at a loss. The old lady had surely got confused about her niece's men-friends.

But she hadn't. 'I suppose you're like the rest of the young folk and can't see any wrong in that Damien Eldridge,' she went on, rather sadly. 'But he can't fool a woman of my age. He's a dreadful young man, and I've put a great deal of money into that film company of his. So has my niece Margaret, and as she's determined to marry him, well, I suppose I shouldn't say anything. But I can't help wishing she'd married Adam Thorne.'

They were at a deadlock then, for Barbara had no words to say to someone who disliked Damien so much. She had had time to recover from her own prick of doubt about him earlier that day, and she had since been accused by Margaret of going away with Damien. Now she was inclined to think that Margaret more than asked for all she got. Barbara was by now inclined to think she had been too harsh in her thoughts of Damien's treatment of Margaret. If Damien could feel the old lady's hostility washing over him, coupled with Margaret's moods, was it likely he would want to come and sit with Margaret and endure more scenes from her?

And so Barbara's thoughts twisted and turned, and her affections went out again to Damien. He wasn't so bad after all, and he would surely do as she asked, if only to please her. To Barbara — sitting there with Margaret's aunt, hearing her talk about her niece as if Margaret were the gentlest and best of creatures — it seemed that Margaret had mesmerised them all, held them in a sort of spell, so that in spite of her ways, she had them all only too anxious to do their best to help her.

It must have been some sort of charm she exerted over all these people! There was Adam Thorne, surely a shrewd man, one not to be taken in by anybody, and here he was ready to be condemning about both Barbara and Damien, just because Margaret couldn't imperiously demand to see anyone just when she was ready. And there was this nice old aunt, too, believing badly of anyone who didn't pander to her niece's slightest whim.

Barbara didn't see Adam Thorne privately the next day, or the day after. He was as courteous as ever to her, when she had occasion to be with him or near him, but he said no more to her about Margaret, nor did he ask if she had done anything about contacting Damien. When she tried to speak to him about it, he said rather coolly, 'Not now, Nurse. Later.'

After making the effort to speak to him for two days, she decided that he was tacitly implying that he believed she had no intention of contacting Damien for Margaret's sake, so she abandoned the effort.

But as she was going off duty at the end of the second day, it struck her that Margaret would see to it that he believed — as she did — that Barbara wanted Damien for herself, and perhaps might even tell Adam Thorne that she privately believed Barbara had been away with him that week-end.

Her cheeks scorched as she thought

of the possibility. Whatever else happened, she couldn't bear him to think
that of her. At all costs, she must find
him, see that it was the right account of
her week-end that was given to him.
She didn't care if he did protest that he
was too busy to talk to her about it. She
must make him listen!

He was coming out as she reached
the main door, and he pulled up short
to light his pipe.

He looked at her over the flame of
the match and again she was made
aware of the strength in that rugged
face of his, and the calm quality. Here
was a man you wouldn't shift easily
from a conviction, once it had taken
root in his mind. For one moment she
was on the verge of quailing, not even
trying to explain to him the truth. Let
him think she had been away with
Damien if he must! It might be
preferable to putting herself in the
invidious position of trying to deny it
and failing.

Then the match went out. He threw

the stalk away and she saw he was smiling at her. 'Hallo, where are you off to? I was just coming to look for you!' he said.

He was the most infuriating man for sheer unpredictable moods, she told herself.

'I was going out for a walk, Mr. Thorne, but there was something I remembered wanting to tell you.'

'Then we'd better walk together,' he said, his eyebrows raised. 'That's if you can bear my dull company!'

She looked so surprised that he laughed, a short, rueful bark of a laugh. 'After the polished charm of your friend Eldridge, I meant,' he added.

He didn't sound very much amused. Displeased, rather, she thought, and hastened to make her explanation now, since he had introduced the subject so soon.

'I suppose that means you've been up to see Miss Knowles,' she began.

'I have, but I don't see — '

'That's what I wanted to explain.

When I saw her last, I told her Mr. Eldridge had gone away for a few days to recuperate, and that I'd been away with a friend over the week-end and that was how it was I hadn't been to visit her. She jumped to the conclusion that the friend I had mentioned was Mr. Eldridge.'

He looked down into her distressed, indignant young face and he looked very angry indeed. Never had she seemed quite so young and vulnerable and . . . he searched for the word and found it. *Unprotected.* He wanted to protect her, from everything and everyone, particularly the Margaret Knowles of this world, and their lashing tongues.

'I'm sure you're mistaken,' he said quickly. 'Margaret would never think such a thing.'

'I didn't think you'd believe it,' she said dully. 'But her aunt was there and heard her say it. She'll tell you. I don't mind very much what Miss Knowles believes about me — it's you. I didn't want you to think I'd been away with him,' she finished, with a little rush.

'Why? Does it matter to you what I believe about you?' he asked, trying to sound disinterested for fear of betraying his own feelings. Sometimes he feared that this girl and everyone else must be well aware of how very much interested he was becoming in her: he, who had been an avowed woman-hater since that business with Margaret over a year ago!

'Well, of course it does! It isn't true — it never could be true, and I'd hate you to think such a thing of me!' she burst out. 'Besides, I spent quite a lot of time trying to find him and even now I can't contact him until he returns, because no one knows where he is exactly. He wanted so badly to be left alone to get fit again.'

'And to be well beyond the reach of any calls from the hospital about Margaret,' Adam remarked dryly. 'Elusive gentleman, isn't he?'

She didn't argue with that. She herself was rather cross with Damien for not letting her know about this. It had made her feel so silly when she had telephoned the people at the film studios. They had been helpful, yet at the same time there had been an underlying note in their voices which had suggested to her that it was no new thing for Damien to slide off somewhere leaving no address, while young women came on the telephone wanting to know where he was. He might at least have said good-bye to her and told her he was going away.

'What did you want to speak to me about, Mr. Thorne?' she asked, remembering he had said he was looking for her.

'Let's find somewhere more quiet to discuss that — what's the time? Yes, we've got time to run out to Kearney Cross and back. I'll bring my car round, if you'd like to wait here.'

He was the oddest person, she thought. No one would believe that he had been so cool and aloof with her since she had returned from her week-end off! He was almost friendly again!

He brought the car round and waved to her. When she had climbed in, he drove round the back of the hospital and took the London road out to where Kearney Waters lay glistening in the rising mist.

It was a very lovely spot. They got out and walked on the sandy shore of the lake, each unwilling to break the companionable silence.

Somewhere an owl hooted, and above them a pale crescent of a moon rode in a clear sky, but across the gently lapping water a thick pearly mist was creeping after the unseasonal warmth of the day.

'Have you been here before?' Adam asked her suddenly.

'No. I usually spend week-ends with my friend Sue's family. On the farm. This is a beautiful spot.'

'Yes, I thought we might have a little talk here without interruption. It's never easy to apologise for being a perfect bear, but that's what I'm about to do.'

He seemed to delight in taking the wind out of her sails. She was covered in confusion.

'Oh, please don't,' she stammered. 'After all, you're entitled to — I mean, we all know you're worried about Miss Knowles!'

He shook his head. 'It's something about you that makes me like that,' he said, after staring at her in silence. 'There are times when I — well, there are times when I want to shake you, and then I'm confoundedly sorry afterwards. How old are you, by the way?'

'How old do you think I am?' he startled her into asking.

'Common sense tells me you must be over eighteen, to become a nurse, but there are times when you look no more than sixteen and I'm tempted to believe you lied about your age to get admitted.'

'Sixteen! I don't know whether to be

flattered or dismayed. I'm twenty-two,' she said, laughing.

She always looked younger than her age in mufti, she was well aware. She hadn't a flair for dress like some of the young nurses. Tonight she had put on a pale blue sweater over a kilted skirt, and she wore a short lambswool-lined suede jacket — a practical garment that was intended to stand up to all weathers for a long time to come, because she hadn't a lot of cash to spare on clothes.

He took all this in, standing there looking at her as if he had never seen her before, and although she couldn't hope to know it, he was filled with a mounting rage at the effrontery of Damien Eldridge, who thought he could add this lovely, untouched girl to his list of women-friends.

'Does it matter how old I am?' she asked gently, still rather puzzled.

'D'you know how old I am?' he asked, by way of reply.

'Goodness, Mr. Thorne, I never gave it a thought!'

He should have been prepared for that, but he wasn't. It made him feel older than ever, and more out of the running.

'How old is Eldridge?' he asked gruffly.

'But everyone knows that! Oh, I suppose you wouldn't — I mean,' she added hastily, conscious of always saying the wrong thing to him, 'I mean you probably don't read the film magazines as I and my friends do. He's twenty-four, actually.'

'And from that source you have also discovered his background, his tastes, everything about him?'

'Um,' she murmured, staring dreamily across the lake and smiling a little. 'We talk about him. We see all his films. He's — well, the sort of man-friend every girl dreams about, I suppose. Sauve, charming, good-looking, and although he looks so young, he's got self-confidence and experience. Those things do count, you know.'

'Apparently!' he said, drily.

'Some of my friends went so far as to write for his autographed photograph and frame it for their dressing-tables — only to be got out after Home Sister's round each night, of course. But I never went as far as sending for his picture.'

'Why?'

'I don't know. I suppose because it's the typical act of a film fan. If I couldn't meet him and get to know him personally, I didn't want to be just a fan.'

'And now you have met him personally. Does he measure up to your dreams about him?'

'More so, because he seems a real person, not the popular conception of a film star! At least, that was how it was until I telephoned the studios and asked for his address to contact him for Miss Knowles.'

'What happened to knock your idol down?'

'It didn't knock him down,' she said slowly, trying to put her thoughts into words. 'He's a very nice person. You can't possibly know that until you meet him. He's gentle, and he doesn't want to talk about himself all the time, he listens to the other person.'

She was still staring over the lake so she missed Adam's cynical lift of the eyebrow at that.

'Perhaps it was the atmosphere of the studios and the way they talked about him,' she went on, 'but it didn't seem the same person they were talking about. It was all rather unreal, and he became unreal, too, although he wasn't there. D'you see what I mean?'

'I do indeed, and perhaps it's as well,' Adam said crisply, his nice new friendliness vanishing. 'Because there is no sense in hurting yourself over someone else's husband-to-be. He's going to marry Margaret, you know, if I (as an old friend of the family and the only man she has, to act in her interests) have to personally hold him to it!'

7

Damien telephoned Barbara at the hospital a week later. He was very gay and said he was all alone in the flat of his friends and they could have a nice little chat.

'The people at the studios said you'd been asking for me, honey! I'm sorry I couldn't let you know where I was going, but I didn't know myself at the time!'

'You could have telephoned when you arrived, couldn't you?' Barbara was moved to point out.

'What, from Scotland? Well, I suppose I could, but I did want to keep it a secret, and I did want to feel cut off — you know what I mean? Real relaxation. Honey, you haven't asked how I am yet,' and he sounded quite hurt.

'Well, how are you?'

'Absolutely fit again, and my leg only troubles me the tiniest bit when it's going to rain! I shall be on the set again in no time!'

'Aren't you going to ask how Miss Knowles is?' Barbara asked quietly.

There was the smallest pause, then he dutifully asked how Margaret was.

'She collapsed when she heard you'd left the hospital without even letting her know you were going!' Barbara said.

He thought quickly, and acted quickly enough to almost deceive Barbara, leaving her unsure whether it was the truth or not. 'But I left a note for her! Didn't that idiot deliver it? Oh, really, you can't trust anyone to see to a thing!'

If it wasn't the truth, it was the nicest bit of acting over the telephone that Barbara had ever heard. But then, of course, acting was his business, and somehow she couldn't be sure that it wasn't acting.

'No one seemed to know anything about a note from you! Anyway, it would have been kinder to go up and say a few words, wouldn't it, Damien? After all, you hadn't seen her since the accident, had you?'

She held her breath. Why did she have to say that? She knew he would be angry, and she didn't want to annoy him. It was true what Adam Thorne had said — Damien did still belong to Margaret and Barbara had no right to feel like this about him. But she did, and her heart was hammering madly with excitement at hearing him on the other end of the line, even though he was only defending himself about his attitude towards Margaret.

'Honey, we can't discuss this on the telephone,' he said at last. 'When can we meet? I've been thinking of you all the time I've been away, and now I'm back I don't want to quarrel with you before I can even get a sight of that precious face of yours!'

'Then come over to the hospital and see Miss Knowles,' Barbara said quickly. She had promised Adam

Thorne, and she must keep that promise, to try to get Damien here. 'They want to operate on her, but she's working herself up because she can't see you! Don't you understand?'

'She'll be a jolly sight worse if she sees me,' he said gloomily. 'She'll throw such a scene, everyone will wish I'd never come back! So what good will it do?'

'Will you come, and we'll take that risk?' Barbara insisted.

'All right, I'll come,' he said quietly. 'But not today. I've only just arrived, and frankly after that journey, I hardly feel — '

'You promise to come tomorrow? Can we send an ambulance for you?'

'Really, Barbara!' he exploded, then he quickly turned to laughter. 'Sweet, you are so thoughtful, but I assure you, it won't be necessary. I can be driven over from Maplefield, but there is something you can do!'

'What is it?'

'I wish you'd pop over here tonight

and brief me as to what's going on with Margaret. I can't talk over the phone any longer — I'm not alone any more. There are things I must know, so will you come?'

'I'm not sure,' Barbara stammered. 'It isn't your flat, is it? Besides — '

'Listen, I shan't be here alone if that's what you're thinking, but we can find a quiet spot to talk. Tell you what — I'll ask them to send a car for you, when you come off duty. How's that? And be an angel, don't come in uniform. It'll make me feel I'm in hospital again!'

There were voices in the background, calling to him, so Damien hastily said good-bye to Barbara and rang off before she could say any more.

She was trembling all over. Furiously she took herself to task about it. Was she going to be like the rest of her set, and go like a jelly at the thought of seeing the film star, not as his nurse in hospital, but as a guest in his producer's flat?

Sternly she reminded herself that she was simply going, as usual, as emissary for Damien's fiancée. She went to find Adam Thorne, to tell him she had achieved a promise from Damien to come the next day, but Adam had gone off duty.

Sue wasn't at their meal, either, so Barbara had no one to talk to about it. She thought about going up to Margaret to tell her and to cheer her up, but some inner instinct cautioned her to wait until Damien actually arrived. It would be terrible if anything prevented him from coming at the last moment.

Barbara swiftly changed into the same clothes she had worn when Adam drove her to Kearney Cross. After all, it was only a call on a previous patient, to brief him about visiting another patient. Yet when she was settled in the rather grand car, with the elaborately uniformed chauffeur at the wheel, she was sorry she hadn't put on something more formal. The man was very sweet and kind but, like Adam, he must have thought she was only sixteen. That was how he treated her, anyway, and it depressed Barbara.

The man drove smoothly through the streets of Hopwood, out into the open country and into the better residential part of Maplefield, stopping at last in the small private road belonging to one of the largest new blocks of luxury flats. Then he personally escorted Barbara across a hall which seemed miles wide, carpeted with something that felt like foam mattresses under her feet. There was a gilt self-working lift, and he took her up in this, and delivered her to a door that was partly ajar.

'Oh, no, this can't be the place!' Barbara protested. 'There seems to be a party going on in this flat!'

'That's right,' the chauffeur agreed kindly. 'It's a welcome home party for Mr. Eldridge. This way, miss,' and she was firmly taken inside and handed over to a white-coated manservant who stripped her of the lambswool-lined coat, and left her feeling overdressed in a room of women in dresses that revealed yards of bare arm, oceans of bare back, and so much glitter that it hurt the eyes.

The noise hurt the ears, too. Noise from beat music, the shuffle of many feet on the polished floor, the hum and chatter of many voices and the odd isolated high-pitched laugh. There was such a crush, such a suffocating smell of mingled perfumes, cigar smoke, cigarette fumes and whisky, that Barbara felt she wanted to turn tail and run out into the fresh air.

Then the hostess bore down on her and said something. What she said was lost in the din going on around. The hostess shrugged helplessly, rolled her eyes to the ceiling, and taking Barbara's hand, pulled her through the crush to a door on which a label had been hung: 'Girls'. The door next to it had a label reading 'Boys'. So this, Barbara thought, with the first pangs of a headache coming on, was what a film star's party was like!

Inside the bedroom, however, it was comparatively quiet. A redhead sat before a dressing-table's wing mirrors, carefully applying a pencil to her eyebrows. The hostess said, looking Barbara over carefully, 'Oh, very nice! So you're Damien's latest! Well, well! One never knows what to expect next, but still, it makes a change!'

'Oh, no, I'm one of the nurses from the hospital,' Barbara said hastily. 'I didn't know it was to be a party! The idea was to come over and talk to Damien — somewhere quiet, he said.'

'Did he! Thank your stars there *is* a party on, dear, when he's in that mood! Though heaven knows, it doesn't make much difference, whether there's a party or not, sometimes!'

'I meant he said it would be quiet to talk although there would be other people here,' Barbara corrected, but she could feel the colour rushing up her cheeks at her hostess's implication.

'Well, anyway, now you're here, if you

want to tidy up — I'll find you a drink when you're ready. I'm Clare,' the hostess said. 'Dawn will help you, won't you, dear?'

Dawn stopped doing things to her eyebrows and stared at Barbara in the mirror. 'Like Romany, isn't she?' she said at last.

Clare had a good look at Barbara then. 'Yes, she is, now you come to mention it. At least, like Romany when she's playing the juvenile lead.'

'Well, that's what I meant,' Dawn agreed, and returned to her make-up.

'Look, I don't really want to tidy. I just want to say a few things to Damien, and then I'll go,' Barbara urged.

'Oh, but you must have a drink first,' Clare said.

'Well, if you don't want to tidy, then you don't, so let's go. Oh, one word, honey — I wouldn't get into a huddle with Damien if I were you, not at this party, I mean. You see, Romany's here, and Buck's jealous. He can't help it.

144

He's her husband.'

'Honestly, you've got it all wrong!' Barbara said, in exasperation. 'Damien's engaged to a patient in the hospital. I just came to talk to him about her, arrange about him going to see her tomorrow. How this concerns your friend Romany and her husband, I can't think! Do find Damien for me, will you? I'll wait here.'

'No, not here, dear — this room's for girls only,' Clare laughed, and unexpectedly Dawn started to laugh too.

Barbara grimly followed Clare out into the main body of the party, where the dancing had now stopped and the noise was even more terrific than before.

Someone thrust a filled glass into Barbara's hand and someone else pushed against her and spilt most of it, narrowly missing Barbara's skirt.

And then Damien materialised. A Damien so alien that for the moment Barbara hardly recognised him.

He had his arm round a little dark

girl in a sheath dress of some dark shiny material that looked a bit like leather, a little like the rippling skin of a seal. The girl moved like that, too, and her lithe young body was as straight down as a baby seal's. Damien looked impatient at being dragged away from her by Clare's insistent hand on his arm.

And then he recognised Barbara. 'Darling! Didn't you dress? Did I forget to mention it was a party? Oh, I want my head searching,' and he kissed her lightly, impersonally, on her cheek. 'Let me introduce you to some people. You've met Clare, and this is — '

'Not now, Damien! I just want to talk to you then I have to get back!' Barbara said desperately.

She gave up saying it after one or two more attempts. Damien, a svelte stranger in his dark blue evening clothes, abandoned the little dark girl, and took Barbara around. She drank a cocktail she didn't like (mainly because it was more simple to drink it than to try to make everyone understand that she didn't want it) and she automatically took small appetising things to eat off a proffered tray, so that the tray should be removed. She was shifted into a corner by the sway and press of many bodies, and by the guiding impulse of Damien's arm round her. Once in the corner, his body shielding her from other people, she said fiercely, 'Why didn't you tell me it was to be a party?'

'Honestly, darling, I didn't know myself!' he protested, and she was forced to believe him. 'When I put the telephone down, someone said something about a surprise, and then it was too late to do anything. Well, what do you care — you look very nice in that thing — ' and she saw that for the first time he was really looking at her, at the simple sweater and pleated skirt, and that he was faintly horrified.

She supposed that most of the women here, when not in their exaggerated party wear, wore tights and leather tops.

'Well, you look very nice,' he said again, this time more firmly, as if to make himself believe it.

That was when the diversion came. The noise subsided for a minute, and Barbara saw that the door had opened to admit two people. Over everyone's heads, by tip-toeing, she could see a big, pallid, fat man, with dark glasses on, dark hair thinning on top, an expensive cigar clamped between his teeth. He swept the room with an unsmiling glance and raised one hand by way of greeting. The woman with him looked very much like Barbara herself at that distance, except that she had on a glittering dress of pale blue sequins.

'Hi, Romany! Hi, Buck!' everyone shouted, and higher pandemonium than before broke out.

'You must meet the director and his wife,' Damien said, helping to push a way through the crush.

'Ought you to be in a party like this?' Barbara protested. 'You ought to take it easy for a bit!'

148

Damien caught what she said, and a frown of irritation fled over his face, but he quickly replaced it with that brilliant smile of his.

'Not to worry!' he said, reaching the new arrivals with something like triumph.

'Damien!' Romany screamed, and threw her arms round his neck, but she only kissed his cheek, and instantly referred him to her husband. 'Buck, Damien's back! Isn't it good to see him again? Honey, we've missed you! Buck was only saying today, weren't you, Buck — '

Her words were drowned by a growl from Buck, who put his hands on Damien's shoulders, and slapped his back and said it was good to see him back and that Romany had only been saying so that very day.

Then they saw Barbara, and for a moment their wide smiles wavered.

'This is the honey I told you about, Buck, remember?' Damien said. 'Now wouldn't she do for that part, *you* know?'

'Yes, wouldn't she just?' someone else put in.

People were pressing all around, pushing Barbara closer to Romany and her husband.

'Honey, you and I ought to get together and do something to that face of yours. It's all undressed,' Romany said.

'Yes, Romany's wizard with make-up,' someone else said.

'Gosh, did you ever see a pan without anything?' another girl said in wonderment, but an effeminate young man by her side said, thinking, 'I don't know. She's got something. Yes, she's definitely got something. I like it. It needs a little pink on the lips, but that's all. Yes, she's got something!'

And all the time Buck Tragman was saying he wanted to talk to Barbara about what work she had already done and the studios she had worked in, and no one listened when she tried to tell them she hadn't, and that she was a nurse from the hospital and had to go soon.

It was a nightmare, that party. The crowd thinned out a little into another room, where there was a buffet. Romany Tragman drifted over to Barbara once or twice to say something, but she wasn't thinking about what she was saying; she was intent on looking at Barbara, at the way she walked, as if she wanted to remember Barbara to recognise her again. It was uncanny. Barbara didn't like it.

She didn't like so many things about that party. The way everyone ostentatiously showed Buck Tragman and his wife how important they were; the way Buck Tragman kept watching his wife; the way Damien seemed so elusive, not like the young man she had known and liked in hospital; most of all the way a philandering type called Russell Mallory, kept drifting over and looking at Barbara, as if he were undressing her.

'Don't mind, kid, he can't help it! It's his way,' a pert little girl said, in the bedroom a little later, as she readjusted her blonde wig.

'He has a reputation to keep up,' her friend giggled. 'You don't have to mind him, but someone else ought to!'

'Romany would be worried if he didn't,' another girl chipped in.

'I'd be careful what you say about her if I were you, honey,' the girl in the blonde wig said. 'That's if you want to keep on the right side of Buck and get a part some day.'

And so it went on. The innuendos about Romany's unfaithfulness, her husband's jealousy, his need to be courted for the sake of a part. Barbara, sickened, disgusted, said at last when she found Damien again, 'I have to go now. Will you promise me to come to the hospital tomorrow?'

He looked at her as if he didn't know her for a moment, then he said, 'Oh, Barbara! How you do keep on, dear! Tomorrow's a long way off, and it's early yet!'

'Damien, I've got to be in by eleven.

Can someone run me back, or is there a bus? I don't know Maplefield!'

Damien thought for a minute, then he said, 'All right, get your coat and we'll go down. I want to speak to you, anyway.'

They slipped away unnoticed and then she found he had taken her out of another entrance and they were on a quiet staircase. Its stone treads, uncarpeted, were the first plain simple sight that had met her eyes in all that lush, disagreeable evening.

'Oh, it's heavenly cool and quiet here!' she said, flinging back her head.

Damien, too, seemed different, now that he was away from his friends. He took her hand.

'Honey, this has been a wretched evening for you and it isn't what I'd planned at all. Yes, yes, I know, you want me to promise to go to the hospital tomorrow. I've said I will and I will. I always keep my word. But let's talk about you.'

'What about me?'

'I mean it, about a screen test. All right, so you don't want to do Margaret out of her cherished ambition. What if I tell you it's another part I've got in mind for you? Does that make it any different?'

'Oh, Damien, I'm a nurse. I don't know how to do anything else, and I'm not sure I'd want to, if it's going to be like that up there tonight.'

'Poor sweet, you didn't like it! It was most unfortunate, pitching you into a noisy crowd like that, first go! It isn't always like that, I assure you! Sometimes it's quite good fun. You must come again, to a nice party. Not like this. But about the screen test — '

'No, Damien, not now. I must get back!'

'It's all right, sweetie! There's plenty of time. The car can take you right to the door. Now don't worry.'

He slipped a friendly, impersonal arm round her shoulders and walked her slowly and reassuringly down flight after flight, talking quietly, reasonably, sensing every inch of the way that she was suspicious of his intentions on this obvious service flight of stairs, and acting the part of his life in reassuring her.

All the time, every fibre of his being urged him to take her into his arms. Out of the hospital, the uniform discarded, she was infinitely desirable. Without make-up she could still look beautiful, and to his jaded view her unspoiled air was like water to a parched traveller in the desert. Yet he dare not let her know. She was a fiery little soul when she was upset, he knew.

'Now about the screen test, when you were in the bedroom the kids were all talking about it. They couldn't get over you! Honestly, they'd seen nothing like it! Even in that simple outfit and no make-up, you could knock most of them cold! They said so!'

'They? You mean that horrid Russell Mallory, I suppose? I know — he told me. And I'd rather not know how he feels about me.'

'Oh, take no notice of him. He doesn't mean any harm. He's played the part so often in pictures, he's forgotten what the real him is like!'

'How dreadful! And is that the sort of thing you want me to leave a nursing career for?'

'Big money, gay times, everyone adoring you?' He was amazed that she didn't yearn for all that.

'I didn't mean that. I meant, supposing I had to continually play a nasty part — might I not identify myself with it in the end, as you say Russell Mallory has?'

'Barbara, honey, you're so sweet . . . ' he said huskily.

They had reached the bottom of the stairs on the ground floor. Away to the left the stairs swooped to the dark basements. There was a door behind her, leading she hoped, to the street. She pushed away from Damien, uncertainly, when that door was suddenly whipped open and Buck Tragman stood there, panting a little, from hurrying.

Barbara noticed at once his suspicious stare, but it wasn't until she was at last in the car, being driven back to the hospital, that she realised what it all meant. Why Damien had so cheerfully said, 'Hello, Buck — Barbara's going — I brought her down the quiet way.' Why Buck had smiled lamely, and said, 'That's right, dears, lose no time. There's never enough time. Never enough,' as he ambled away in the direction of the lift going up again.

Her cheeks scorched. She realised then that it was no idle talk. He had possibly caught sight of the back of her head as she had slipped away from the party with Damien, and he had thought it was his wife.

She hated it. Hated the whole thing. The chauffeur, kindly as ever in a big brother sort of way, tucked a rug over her legs. She was shivering, but not from cold. He asked her, too, where she wanted him to drop her.

'Not at the gates,' she said swiftly. 'I'll

tell you when we reach the road leading to the hospital.'

She didn't want anyone to notice her getting out of this car. The mark of that party was on everything, she felt, and she wished she hadn't gone.

But by the time they had swept through the dark lanes, the car's big headlamps picking out the already bare trees and making them look like part of the back-cloth on some enormous stage, she had also drunk in the fresh night air deep into her lungs, and she felt better.

She had never been so glad to see Hopwood again, and never had the massive grey crouching hulk of the hospital building seemed so welcome.

The chauffeur pulled up, as she directed, at the end of the road. Kindly he insisted on waiting there until he had seen her go into the main gates, but he need not have bothered.

She didn't have to walk the length of that half dark road alone. Almost as soon as she had put a yard between her and the opulent car, a familiar voice called: 'Is that you, Nurse Caley? Wait a minute — I'll walk you back!' and Adam Thorne's well-known footsteps came striding along behind her.

8

It was a most uncomfortable walk along that road. Barbara would have been glad enough of Adam Thorne's company in the ordinary way; it was an ill-lit street, with moving shadows under the gaunt trees, between the few scattered lamp-posts.

But tonight it was frankly uncomfortable. Behind her, the chauffeur grimly sat, watching her until she went into the hospital gates; beside her Adam Thorne strode, wrapped in a silence more telling than words.

Once inside the gates, however, they heard the big car start up and slowly purr up the road past them and out of sight. Then Adam Thorne did have a few things to say.

'I take it that that car belonged to Eldridge?' he asked crisply, and he turned into the path that led to the

Nurses' Home, making it quite clear that he intended to use the next five minutes' walk in getting what information he wanted.

Passionately she didn't want him to walk her right up to the front door of the Home, but he was the Casualty Officer. He had a right to do so if he wished.

'Yes, it was,' she said, rather more heatedly than she had meant to. 'It was only right that he should provide transport back from Maplefield for me, don't you think?'

She forget he didn't know the significance of Maplefield, but he quickly reminded her.

'I'm sorry. I thought I told you,' she said at once. 'He was to stay there at the flat of some other film people, when he returned from Scotland.'

'I thought you didn't know where he was?' he was quick to take her up.

'I didn't. He telephoned me late today. He'd just arrived and he was too tired to visit the patient then.'

'But not too tired to make a date with you. Where have you been tonight?'

They were too near the lighted windows of the Home for comfort. She turned and faced him.

'I've been to the flat where he's staying,' she said.

'What, alone with him?'

'No. With about fifty other people. I still don't know how they packed them all in.'

'Fifty other — you mean to say he was giving a party?'

'Mr. Thorne, I'm trying to tell you what happened. He said on the telephone that he wanted to talk quietly about the patient, be briefed in fact for a visit he proposed to make to Miss Knowles tomorrow. He asked me to go over there in the car he would send, for a quiet talk. He assured me there were only the people he was staying with, in the place, and that they wouldn't bother us.'

'Very nice! And you believed that!

You want looking after! Don't you realise what danger you might have run into?'

'I don't see why you're being so angry and difficult with me,' she burst out, her caution leaving her, as her headache and weariness grew. 'Apparently his friends fixed up a surprise party to welcome him home, without his knowledge. It was crowded and stuffy and hideously noisy. I hated every minute of it, and if I'd known it was going to be like that, I wouldn't have gone — not even for you!'

'For me! That's a good one! When have I asked you to go to one of Eldridge's parties, I'd like to know?'

'You did ask me to fix up with him to see the patient. I've been trying to do just that for well over a week now. You know that! And this was the only way I could see to achieve it. He's promised me he'll come tomorrow. Well, that's what you wanted, isn't it?'

He stood looking down at her, and suddenly he smiled, that rather rueful smile she was coming to know so well.

'I suppose I deserved that. All right. I'm very sorry. I thank you very much for all your efforts, even if the blighter doesn't come. Am I forgiven?'

'Oh, there's nothing to forgive,' she said, sorry too. 'I'm sorry I flared out. I shouldn't have, but I'm like a fish out of water at that sort of party. Everyone had on scintillating dresses and jewellery and make-up and scent and I was only wearing this. I didn't know it was to be a dress-up evening.'

'You look very nice as you are. I, for one, wouldn't want you to change, ever. And I don't care to think of you in that sort of gathering, either. Look, your free time's been taken tonight and at other times — let me make it up. Yes, really, I'd like to. A quiet little party on our own. What do you say? How about Saturday night. I'm off early, and I don't think you'll be late, will you?'

'But will it be a dress-up party?' she asked, rather childishly, as she hastily reviewed in her mind her meagre wardrobe.

'No. Oh, no. Just wear the nicest dress you have. I'll just put on a dark suit, and try to look respectable for once. Meet you outside with the car, say sevenish? Now you'd better pop off inside or you'll have Home Sister after me. And thanks — thanks a lot for everything!'

She hurried into the Home, her mind in a whirl. She felt curiously shaken and wondered why she had agreed to go out with him.

It was very strange. No matter how much excitement she felt about Damien Eldridge, her reaction to Adam Thorne was much more upsetting, in a different way.

After Home Sister had made her round, Barbara couldn't sleep, and got up to stand at the window, looking out on to the gardens of the hospital.

Across the bare trees, the lights of the hospital still shone; brilliantly where the theatre block was, more subdued where the wards were — but it was there, the friendliest thing in her life, and the only home she had. It offered, too, the only security she had, and she clung to it.

Beyond it were the two unknown quantities, tugging at her perpetually; Damien Eldridge and Adam Thorne.

She understood neither the two men, nor her own personal feelings where they were concerned, and not so long ago neither of them made any serious impact on her quiet life, and she had been at peace then. Happy, tranquil.

Now she didn't know what she was, and it all started on her first day in Casualty, when she had met Adam Thorne and heard about his unhappy love affair, and later that day she had met the girl, Margaret Knowles, and swiftly in her wake, Damien Eldridge, the film star Barbara had dreamed about for so long.

A shattering day, and its repercussions were like the ripples in a pond, round a stone that has been flung in.

Damien was like two people; he still

belonged to Margaret, but was fighting to get away from her, and he clearly showed that his thoughts were turning to Barbara. But he had been a different person in hospital; that man, in the hospital bed, away from his friends and his film background, had been the one who had caught her imagination, sent her heart soaring and lent wings to her feet. Now the man he was in the film world, left her perplexed and miserable.

And Adam Thorne? Here was a problem, and danger. She sensed the danger underlying his association with her, without understanding it. It wasn't the kind of danger to make her afraid, so much as the sort of danger that was making the ground slide away from beneath her feet. With his strength and experience, his seniority over her, both in years and position, he often haunted her dreams as a great rock that had to be scaled or got round or . . . accepted. A curious dream that repeated itself in many ways. It struck her now, that he occupied too large a part in her consciousness. He was always there, in the background, now smiling, tender, kind, now angry, that thunderous look making her heart beat urgently, unevenly.

They had said of him that he was even in temperament, uninterested in women since Margaret had jilted him. From Barbara's experience of him, he seemed a very normal man with a normal man's swift anger, swifter delight, and . . . if he had been anyone else, and she herself had been someone else, she might even have thought that he was showing common or garden jealousy of her association with Damien.

But in his case it was absurd. Why should Adam Thorne be jealous of her friendship with Damien? No, rather he was angry at her apparent lifting of Damien from Margaret Knowles.

Barbara shrugged helplessly, and went back to bed, conscious that her feet were cold, and that a new sensation of vague unhappiness was taking possession of her. She didn't really want Damien, she saw, with growing uneasiness. Yet she couldn't have told herself why, nor indeed what it was that she did want. Yet the rising yearning in her was becoming too big a thing to be denied.

She told herself impatiently that it was because she was tired and not very warm, and worried. Worried about Margaret Knowles and whether Damien would keep his promise and come the next day. She went to sleep at last to dream that she was being tossed into a lake — Kearney Waters. Damien had thrown her in, Adam was the one who was diving to rescue her. She awoke without finding out what happened, and the unhappiness and yearning of the night before were still very much with her.

Yet that day went very well. Damien did keep his promise and come to visit Margaret. There were no scenes. Damien behaved beautifully, Barbara heard, and Margaret appeared to be quite happy in the belief that he loved her and had been prevented from actually visiting her by various good reasons so far.

Everyone was talking about it. The surgeons were satisfied that they could now go ahead with the operation, so great was the improvement in the mercurial Margaret's condition. The operation was scheduled for Saturday morning.

Barbara heard no word from Damien that day, nor the next. He was an astute young man and he had sensed that the party had been a mistake. He had known all about it, and had thought that the glamour of it would react on Barbara as it could be expected to react on any young girl who had no glamour at all in her life. He had expected her to capitulate, regarding the screen test, and allow them to rush her off her feet. Now he saw that he had to think again.

No, the film background clearly

didn't appeal to her. What was it she wanted?

As with a new part, he tried to put himself into Barbara's skin. Seen through her eyes, her life horrified him. The life of the hospital struck him as sordid, but he recognised that he was infatuated with her and her unspoiled air. He had to admit, too, that it was no fake, as he had tried to persuade himself at first. She was, he now admitted, genuinely unspoiled, and he wanted her. He wanted her with a fierceness that frightened him.

The thing was to please her, and to that end, he went to the hospital to visit Margaret, and did the thing properly as only he could. Then he turned his attention to Barbara and her own tastes. Music — good music. She had once told him, while he was in hospital, that her ambition was to own a fine radiogram and a record library. Well, that could be supplied, here in his friend's flat.

He went at once to the telephone, to call Barbara up and invite her over for a quiet evening.

Barbara wasn't available and Sue took the message. He had met Sue. All girlish enthusiasm about the film world and himself. A nice conventional girl, easy to understand, but annoyingly protective about Barbara.

He wasn't surprised when Barbara came on the telephone later, and told him in no uncertain terms that she didn't want to visit him in anyone's flat for a quiet evening.

'Bar, honey, how unkind of you to be suspicious! That was not what was in my mind at all!' he chided.

'What wasn't?' she returned swiftly.

'Whatever it was that you thought I meant by a quiet evening, and which you didn't like the sound of,' he retorted.

She had to chuckle, but as she pointed out: 'I can't spend any sort of evening with you now, and you should know that!'

'I've missed the point, darling. Why not now?'

'Because of Margaret Knowles,' she said patiently. 'You're engaged to her, remember? And now you've been to see her and it's all right between you both — '

'You can't win!' he broke in with an exasperated sigh.

'Look, honey, you wanted me to go to the hospital, and I did it, to please you! Now you seem to think that bars me from seeing you any more!'

'You didn't mean it? You just visited her to please me?' she cried in dismay. 'Oh, *no*!'

'Now what's the matter?'

'Margaret thinks you love her!'

'All right, so she thinks that. I can't help it. I did my best to please you (and incidentally everyone else) and what Margaret thinks is beside the point. You don't know her very well, sweetie, or you wouldn't go on like this. She knows perfectly well I don't want to marry her any more. She's just playing up, and having got me there playing the perfect lover, she's tied me nicely down in the eyes of everyone (she thinks!) and that pleases her. But that's all there is to it, I assure you. When she's well again, I'm pulling out, and no one can blame me. Now — when am I going to see you again, sweetie?' he finished. 'How about Saturday?'

'No, I can't, honestly. I've got a date then.'

'Oh.' That put him out. He had thought of her as completely unattached, his for the taking. 'Look, scrap the idea of coming to the flat. I do understand your objection to that. It was stupid of me. What about a nice sedate dinner at a nice sedate hotel, and a walk on the beach afterwards? I know just the place!'

'I can't — ' she began, but he broke in.

'Just beyond Saxonbarn,' he urged. 'A darling unspoilt little place called Bride's Bay. You'd love it. Near enough to the main Saxonbarn road to run you back to the hospital in good time afterwards. What do you say?'

'I can't on Saturday — honestly!'

'Then make it Sunday!' he pressed.

'All right,' she said, caving in suddenly. It was time she came off the telephone, and the flashing white of a nurse's apron appeared along the corridor. She could see it out of the corner of her eye. 'Yes, I mean it. I'll come,' she said.

'Then I'll be there, outside the gates, seven sharp.'

Barbara rang off with a sigh, and found Sue at her elbow. 'Was that Damien Eldridge?' she asked, frowning.

'Yes, I thought I'd call him up and get it over!'

Barbara said. 'Gosh, look at the time! I must fly!'

'But you told him you'd be there,' Sue protested.

'You're never going, Bar?'

'Yes, why not?' Barbara said, hurrying away.

Colin Price came along. 'What's wrong, Sue?'

'It's Bar. She must be off her head. I ought to tell her. That Damien Eldridge rang her to date her, and I heard her tell him she'd be there, but she can't realise — he was suggesting a cosy evening alone with him in someone's flat, with records!'

'How do you know, Sue?' Colin asked her.

'Because he rang up before and she wasn't available so he gave the message to me!'

Colin shook Sue's arm. 'Snap out of it, Sue! It can't be that — Barbara's a nice girl. Besides, what could you do about it? She's over twenty-one!' He laughed. 'Jealous? Because she's dating a film star and you're stuck with a dresser?'

'All right, it's none of my business,' Sue laughed. 'But just the same, it always used to be, only just lately we're not so close. At home last week-end, she didn't have nice cosy heart-to-hearts with me like she used to. She's . . . living in a world all her own these days.'

'I trust you don't have heart-to-hearts with her either,' Colin said severely, 'if heart-to-hearts means discussing your current bloke. Personally I wouldn't like to be the subject of a cosy bed-time chat by two of you nurses!'

Sue forgot her anxiety about that phone call, however, because Barbara — with an eye to her neglected paper work of late — stayed in the next few nights and studied.

Saturday, with the operation, came at last. It was a subject that interested almost everyone. It wasn't every day that people involved in an accident came from the film world, and the thought that a film career might have been nipped in the bud through careless driving, caught everyone's imagination. No-one blamed Margaret, oddly enough; instead, it seemed that almost everyone was awaiting the outcome of that operation, hoping it would set her on the way to recovery so that the plastic surgery on her face could be begun.

Barbara had the day off. After working late for several nights, she was glad of a leisurely stretch of hours before going out. Deliberately she had forced herself to put the thought of Adam Thorne out of her mind. It made her uneasy, the way excitement gripped her at the thought of dinner with him. She didn't know what to expect of him now, the way he had climbed down on that last occasion.

Because she was also being taken out on the Sunday by Damien, she had thought it worth while to dip into her savings for a new dress for both occasions, and she was out shopping when Sue came to find her to tell her of the outcome of Margaret's operation.

She herself was going out with Colin, and couldn't wait any longer. When Barbara arrived back, she had a leisurely bath and changed. As she had spent so long in the shops choosing this rather important frock, she skipped tea, and so didn't see any of the others to speak to.

At last she was ready. She sauntered out, in good time, to meet Adam Thorne.

Seven o'clock came and went, and as the hands of the big clock in the church tower above the roof-tops, reached twenty past seven, Barbara began to feel uneasy. Adam wasn't the sort of man to be late for a date, she was sure, without letting a girl know. After all, it wasn't far to leave a message at the Nurses' Home.

Puzzled, she decided to go back again and telephone the porter. After all, she had been out most of the day. It was hardly likely that there had been a major accident without her having heard, but he might have been on call for someone else dropping out.

As she waited for the call to be answered, two of the older nurses went through the hall together. She heard them mention Adam Thorne's name, and paused to listen.

'Well, it's all very fine,' one was saying, 'but would he spend most of the afternoon at her bedside if it wasn't true?'

'Personally I never believed it when everyone kept saying he'd got over that old love affair,' the other one agreed.

The porter answered the ringing telephone at last.

Barbara forced herself to think. Her original question was left unasked. Instead, she said, 'Do you happen to know where Mr. Thorne is at this moment?'

'Why, yes, nurse — he's still in Miss Knowles' room,' the porter said without hesitation.

'I see,' Barbara said, flatly. 'No, no message,' and she put the telephone down.

So he was back with Margaret Knowles. He had forgotten all about their date. And everyone knew. Everyone was talking about it. That was what hurt most. They all knew that he still cared for Margaret, and she alone had been fool enough to think he didn't; fool enough to believe him when he had said he just wanted to see Margaret married to Damien Eldridge.

A lump rose in her throat, and scorching tears were pricking behind her eyes. Not until then did she realise how much she had been looking forward to this date with Adam Thorne. It took a knock like that to show you just how much you wanted something.

And as if it wasn't enough that he still hankered for Margaret himself, he was trying to drive a wedge between Barbara and Damien. Goodness, he couldn't have it all ways! How dog-in-the-manger could you get?

Furiously, she dialled Damien's number which he had insisted on giving her, that last time he spoke to her on the telephone. But there was no one there. The telephone kept on ringing and ring-ing.

Well, what did she expect, she asked herself? Her date with Damien was for the Sunday. Why shouldn't he go out tonight?

She came out of the little booth, and crossed the hall to go up the stairs to her room and take off the new frock. She felt she would hate its soft blue folds, from now and for always. The first new frock she had had since she became a nurse, and this had to happen!

Someone came through the swing door and stood on the mat, noisily clearing his throat.

She turned round to see who it was, and there was Damien Eldridge, immaculate in evening dress, smiling half-mischievously, half-ruefully, as if he expected a scolding.

'I've got several good reasons for being here, and I'm not sure which to pick, sweetie, so I think I'll stick to the good old hoary excuse of not remembering whether our date was for tomorrow or tonight!'

She turned and ran down the stairs to him, April tears and smiles mingling.

Because of what had happened tonight, she was more pleased in her greeting than she would otherwise have been.

'Damien!' she cried. 'I don't care what excuse you make for being here, I'm just so glad you're here!'

9

Bride's Bay was a place that Damien would normally have shunned like the plague. It offered nothing for him.

By habit he wore his dark glasses, but he need not have bothered. Bride's Bay was not the sort of place to go wild with delight over the spectacle of a film star dating a girlfriend.

But for Barbara, it was all delightful. The Cliff Hotel — naturally the most expensive in the place or Damien wouldn't have gone there — was noted for its service and fine food and wines, but Barbara loved it because it was designed to cling to the front of the cliffs. Its gardens swooped down in terraces to its own private beach, and the music from the excellent band in the dining-room, was sweet.

Damien acted the part of his life in appearing not only to like it all but to be used to it. 'This,' he confided to Barbara, 'is the real *me*. I hope you really like it and are not just pretending, to please me?'

'But Damien, this is just exactly what I like! I didn't think you liked it, too!' she breathed.

'If you think I really enjoyed that party the other night, you were never more mistaken,' he said, with truth. 'To be honest, I am two people. The person in the film studios, because I have to be: it's my living, my career. But in private life, I don't care for glamour really. And you know, I never thought I'd ever find the girl who liked the same things.' He took her hand across the table, and looked wistfully at her. 'We've never really had much chance of a quiet talk, you and I, and it would be so nice to tell someone all about it — someone who *understood*. I feel you would understand me, Barbara. You make me feel that with you, I could be really *someone*. You know?'

'But you *are* someone, Damien!

You're terribly well-known!' she protested, frowning slightly.

'No, no, I didn't mean that! Of course I'm well-known! All the ballyhoo, the publicity, the public appearances — what do I care about all that? That's nothing to do with me! My publicity agent arranges all that! I just do as I'm told! No, it wasn't that, that I was thinking of.'

'What, then? Tell me!'

The time for confidences came when they had been served, and Barbara had discovered to her delight that by a strange coincidence Damien liked the same food, the same wine. 'But I thought you drank an awful lot of cocktails — that's what your life story disclosed, in one of the magazines,' she protested.

'Oh, that! That's one of the things that makes me very angry,' he told her. 'I'm not like that at all. That's what my publicity agent did for me. He said it would help the box office angle. But I don't think so. You see, Bar sweetie, the way I look at it is, a film star like me is not a private individual but a public person with a service — a *duty* to the public. Do you see what I mean?'

'I think I do,' she said, doubtfully, but he saw he had caught her attention and he let himself go. In the end, so convincing had he been, that he almost believed it all himself, and felt emotionally moved.

'I think of all the thousands of lonely unimportant people who go and sit in the dark to look at me on the screen, and I feel that I ought to *give* them something. I've got this gift of acting, and it isn't for fooling about with or for making big money. No, it's to help people. And so I ask myself — what do they really *need?* All those unattractive women who have no men-friends, it's my job to comfort them, by making them feel for just an hour or so that I *understand* them, that I know that underneath their plain exteriors is a heart of gold!'

Barbara watched him carefully, saying nothing.

'And to all those too old to get boy-friends, it's my job to make them remember how it used to be, or how it *could* have been, if they'd had the luck to meet the Right Man. Sincerity, friendship, kindness, generosity, all those things I have to pour out from the screen, to the old and the lonely, those badly treated, and those too hard up to participate in the goings-on that they see on the screen. It's real acting that's needed to put it across to them, and I feel it's *in me* to do it! And so my life is a constant battle with publicity agents, and the rest of the gang, who just want to portray the glamour, the brittle useless glamour of the screen.'

He was swaying her, so he pushed the point. He also saw that she wasn't used to wine and he surreptitiously kept topping up her glass while he mesmerised her with his talk.

'And when I met you, and felt the blazing sincerity in you, I knew that here was someone who wouldn't want all the outside show of the film world, nor the noisy parties and all that! I saw you as someone like myself, *being* someone important, with a purpose and meaning for all those people who came to see you in pictures. I know you didn't realise that was what I wanted for you, or else you wouldn't have stuck out so hard against a screen test.'

He let the fire die down a little in him. He mustn't overdo it. She was very hard to permanently convince, he saw.

'And that is why, my sweet, I want you to let the idea simmer. Don't put it away from you altogether until you can honestly say to yourself that you've chosen the right vocation. Being a nurse is a wonderful thing, but ask yourself first if you could help people more by bringing truth and colour into their lives, from the screen, than by just putting on a bandage — a job anyone could do?'

He had half convinced her, and he wisely left it at that, contenting himself by adding, 'And if you ever did decide to be an actress, let me assure you that it isn't necessary to be like all those other girls you didn't care for, or even look like them. There are not enough of us daring to be *different* nowadays, and you could be the one, the one person who could dare to be herself, and everyone would be tremendously impressed and *respect* you for it! Don't you ever forget that!'

He danced with her. Conventional ballroom dancing that he sensed she would like. He walked her in the mild air of the sheltered walks on the cliff-face, and they leaned in silence on the rails, listening to the soft lapping of the sea, and watched the myriad stars in the sky. The magic of his personality, his performance, his sense of timing, and the good luck he had had in finding a place and conditions like this, washed over her. She felt healed of the hurt she had sustained, in finding that Adam Thorne had forgotten her.

The mood lasted while they were in Bride's Bay, but when they arrived back in Hopwood, reality descended.

'I forgot to ask you!' she gasped, shocked. 'Have you been on to the hospital today, to find out how Miss Knowles' operation went off? I didn't — I've been out most of the day!'

'That is a thing I don't believe in, pestering the hospital for news before they've got it themselves,' he said smoothly. 'I intend to telephone when I get back to the flat tonight. They'll only say she's progressing satisfactorily, but at least I shall know it's nothing bad.' And again he satisfied her.

Her head was slightly muzzy from the unaccustomed food and drink and sea air, and she wanted her bed. In a way that she didn't quite understand, being out for the evening with Damien was rather a strain. He seemed to demand a certain amount from the other person.

And yet he hadn't kept her out late. She had a midnight pass, but he had carefully got her back at eleven-thirty.

'Now don't let me keep you, sweet.

And don't forget we've a date tomorrow. Same time, same place?'

'Oh, no, this was in place of tomorrow, remember?' she gasped.

'Who says so? You don't seem to realise what sort of place you've got in my life. It's a large one, I assure you!' and with a light squeeze of the hand, he let her go.

Instinct urged her that there was something not quite right about the evening. Beneath the enjoyment and novelty there had been something not quite right.

She would think about it tomorrow, she promised herself, as she stumbled along the darkened path to the Nurses Home.

A man was pacing up and down, smoking a cigarette which he threw away when he saw her coming.

He strode towards her and she saw with dismay that it was Adam Thorne.

'So you've got back, have you? It would have been courtesy to let me know that you were going out with someone else since I couldn't manage it!'

He took her breath away. 'Well, that's the limit!' she stuttered. 'I waited outside for you until seven-thirty and then I telephoned you. Everyone was talking about it and the porter said you were still with her so I concluded you'd forgotten all about me!'

'Do I understand that in spite of my note explaining — '

'What note? I didn't get any note!'

'Nevertheless, I had a note sent over to you, in good time, saying I wouldn't be free until seven thirty, if you'd wait in the Home here,' he said quickly. 'But perhaps you felt that I should have left Miss Knowles, in spite of her critical condition — '

She blanched. 'You mean, the operation didn't go off well?'

'Didn't you know? Didn't you bother to find out?'

'This was my day off. I have been out most of the day,' she said, patiently. 'I'm sorry Miss Knowles isn't so well. How bad is she?'

'Bad enough,' he said abruptly. 'As an old friend, I felt I had to sit with her for a little while, if only in the wild hope that Eldridge might be contacted.'

'Damien!' she said, with a little gasp, putting her hand to her lips. 'He didn't want to worry the hospital with enquiries. He was going to telephone tonight.'

'So you were out with *him*!' She flinched under the bitterness in his tones.

'Well, why not? I'd waited and waited for you and when I heard everyone talking about you being with her, I thought — well, when he turned up, there didn't seem any reason why I shouldn't.'

'I must say I find you difficult to understand, and I think anyone else would, too. Here you have a patient just through from an operation, and just because you are kept waiting by someone who is, after all, a very old friend of the patient, you jump at the first suggestion of an evening out from the very person who should have been at the patient's bedside! Her own fiancé! No, I think that that will need much more explaining away to convince me that it was an accidental meeting or a natural thing to do. It's too late tonight. I'll see you tomorrow, nurse. Goodnight!'

He wouldn't wait, either, to hear anything else that she might have to say.

Again the sense of injustice flooded over her. He was too quick, much too quick, to jump on her, and the fact that she could spend a few hours in Damien's company seemed to him the most heinous of crimes.

She went disconsolately up to her room, and sat on the bed. Her gaze fell on a square of white, half caught under the rug. It was an envelope, stuck in the usual place when someone had flipped it too hard under the closed door.

Scrawled across the corner in pencil was a message: 'Sorry — found it under my door when I got back at ten — that clot of a new maid must have muddled the floors,' and it was signed by the junior in the same room but on the floor above.

Barbara slit it open. It was, of course, from Adam, and it was such a nice friendly note.

'I'm terribly sorry, my dear, but Margaret is in a critical condition and I feel I must stay with her until her aunt arrives. Will try to make it, but expect me to be at least half-an-hour late. Until then, Adam Thorne.'

Such friendliness in writing was a marked change in him, and now they had had another quarrel on top and she had spent the evening in Damien's company!

Whenever she and Adam Thorne appeared to be becoming less frosty to each other, Fate seemed to have a way of stepping in and putting them back where they had been!

The next day, Sunday, Adam was in and out of Margaret's room and there was no opportunity of a talk with him. She did try to tell him she had found his note, but judging from his curt nod to her as he strode by, he hadn't even heard.

Sue, too, was rather peculiar in her manner to Barbara, and when Barbara asked her bluntly what was wrong, Sue shrugged and said: 'If you don't know, there's no point in my trying to tell you!' That sort of remark, Barbara reflected, wasn't designed to help anyone, so she let it go, and in desperation she did what she might not have done otherwise: she went out with Damien again after all.

He had been to the hospital, to visit Margaret, and again he had been the perfect fiancé, so Barbara heard.

Today he said nothing about the film work, the screen test, the people he knew. Cleverly he confined his conversation to the places he was taking her to see. He had discovered cathedral country further inland. She was enchanted to find him ready and willing to escort her around historic places, guide-book in hand, like any tourist in spite of his limp. She had four hours off, and he got her back in nice time to return to duty. In return, she agreed to spend an hour or two with him on the Monday evening, after he had been to see Margaret.

'Black dog for a white monkey,' he chuckled. 'That was what they used to say to me when I was small and liked to make bargains.'

It rather spoiled the outing, to be reminded so pointedly that his attendance on Margaret was merely to secure Barbara's own company, but she turned a blind eye on it. She was doing what she had promised to do for Adam's old friends, purely in the interests of the patient, and if her methods didn't please Adam, she couldn't help it.

That night in her room, Barbara was aware that Sue was keeping away from her. At first, it hadn't been too noticeable. Sue was going around fairly regularly with Colin Price, who, in common with other medical students, had rather odd hours and never knew when he would be on call, so she just threw everything up whenever she was free to be with him. Barbara, too, had been otherwise engaged.

But tonight Sue was in her room. Barbara could hear her moving about, yet she made no attempt to come in and sit on Barbara's bed and tell her about her latest love affair.

Barbara was inclined to feel that perhaps this was the Real Thing at last, with Sue, this affair with Colin Price, and because of that, she wasn't so willing to discuss it with Barbara as she had been about her less important boyfriends.

They had been such close friends at one time that Barbara felt she just had to find out.

Sue opened the door when she knocked softly on the panels.

'Sue, I'm in. You can come for a cocoa if you want to,' she said, lamely, before the wooden expression on Sue's face.

'No, thanks, I don't think I will,' Sue said, after a rather awkward pause. 'I've . . . got things to do.'

'Well, I'll come in and talk to you while you do them then,' Barbara said, edging past her.

Sue shrugged and let her go in, closing the door and standing with her back against it. 'All right, so you want to have it out. I've seen it coming, and you won't like it. You might just as well have left it alone.'

'No, we'd better have it out, whatever it is. I can't go on like this, Sue. What's the matter?'

'Well, you're playing rather a funny game, aren't you? Considering you're supposed to be the non-flirty one of our set, you're surpassing yourself!'

'What does all that mean?' Barbara asked her.

'Oh, come off it, Bar! Everyone's talking about it! You and Damien Eldridge! You know very well he's supposed to be engaged to Margaret Knowles, and she's getting in a fine state because he won't come and visit her!'

'You're a bit late with your news, Sue,' Barbara said wearily. 'That was how it *was*. Thanks to my efforts, he's now visiting her, and he's supposed to have made her happy enough to let them get cracking on the operation.'

'Yes, so happy that she wasn't able to stand up to it, and collapsed after it!' Sue said scathingly.

'That was hardly my fault,' Barbara pointed out gently. 'She's been pretty awful to me one way and another — you forget I go and visit her almost every day — but I've put up with all that, and I've gone to a great deal of trouble to persuade Damien Eldridge to visit her. I do think it's a bit much that people should think I'm trying to get him for myself!'

'It looks very much like it,' Sue said, but with less conviction. 'If I'd been you, I'd have played safe and not gone near him, in the circumstances. You know how people will talk. We're all mushy about him, but that doesn't mean we have to make trouble between him and Margaret Knowles.'

'I'm not making trouble — I'm trying to patch up the trouble which existed before I came into it!'

'Oh, well, if you say so! But I must say it's a bit funny, the way you're going about it!'

'I suppose that means that people have seen that terrible car with the chauffeur at the wheel!' Barbara said, and Sue's face gave away that they had. 'Believe me, it isn't very nice to feel so conspicuous. At least, I didn't find it so. That night I got landed for a very nasty party. I hope it doesn't happen again! And they kept trying to get me to take a screen test. It was horrible.'

'That's one way of describing it,' Sue commented dryly. 'Sounds to me as if you're doing all right for yourself, one way and another!'

'Perhaps it does, but all I can say is,

I'd feel much better if I didn't have to see any of those film people again! Sue, I didn't know they were like that! I've been longing to tell you about it, but you just weren't around.'

She waited to hear what Sue had been doing, but Sue just stood there, still leaning against the door, looking at Barbara as if she were a stranger that she didn't understand at all.

'I know I was as mushy about Damien as the rest of us were,' Barbara went on. 'But I don't think I am any more. At least, sometimes he's very nice, but at other times he's just like the rest of his friends. I don't know, I think I'm rather disillusioned. And he can say what he likes, he does enjoy being a film star and he does like those friends of his! He needn't think he's convinced me otherwise.'

Sue didn't comment on that, either.

'Aren't you going to say anything? Doesn't that satisfy you about what I've been doing?' Barbara cried.

'If you say so,' Sue shrugged.

'Well, what more do you want to know?'

Sue unbent a little then. 'It's so peculiar. I didn't think you were like this. I thought I knew you, Bar.'

'What does that mean?'

'Well, not so long ago, I didn't even know what the Casualty Officer looked like. He was just one of those people you hear about from a distance, a woman-hater and all that. You were asking about him yourself and I did tell you all I'd heard about him.'

'Well, so what?' Barbara asked softly.

'So now he haunts the place, and he's always in a huddle with you, either shouting at you or looking rather nice for someone who's supposed to loathe all women and not even notice mere junior nurses. And they do say you had a date with him last night and ditched him for Damien Eldridge!'

'Oh, that damned grapevine!' Barbara exploded, lying flat on Sue's bed and thumping it with her fists. 'He was going to take me out as a sort of grand reward for jawing my head off, if you'll believe me! I got sick of waiting outside and when Damien turned up and asked me to go out, I was so mad, I went with him. That's positively all!'

But even as she said it, she realised that it wasn't all. It was only part of the truth. It went much deeper than that. She realised then, perhaps for the first time, that it was Adam Thorne that she would really rather be with, and that whatever she had felt for Damien Eldridge in the past was simply the glamour and glitter of the world he represented, and it was fast wearing off. He wasn't even the nice person he had almost convinced her he was. She could see that when she got back to the real life in the hospital and saw everyone and everything in its true perspective.

And it was all too deep and intimate and private to tell Sue, who had somehow stopped being the close friend she had been, and was just one of the ring of lesser friends outside, who was a little too ready to blame, a little unready to accept and understand her motives.

'Well, there it is, Sue,' she muttered, getting up. 'That's all I can tell you. Take it or leave it. How're things with you?'

'So-so.' Sue smiled uncertainly, 'We're only next door and it feels like being on another planet.'

'Me, too,' Barbara nodded, but at that time it seemed impossible to ever bridge the gap again.

Barbara had no intention of seeing Damien any more. That was how she felt when she fell asleep that night. But after a hectic day in Casualty on the Monday, and an accusing stare from Margaret when she had looked in to see her, Barbara was despondent enough to have gone out with any friend who was smiling cheerfully that evening.

And Damien was looking very cheerful. He had virtuously visited Margaret and he felt he was really making some progress with Barbara at last, for there was no mistaking the way her face lit up when she saw him at the open window of that big car of his.

She was in uniform. She had slipped out for a walk. Several of the others of her set had come out, too, in twos and threes. It was a nice evening, crisp and clear, after a humid, half-drizzling sort of day. The others looked curiously at her as she stopped at the car door to speak to Damien.

'You do exaggerate, darling,' he protested. 'I anticipated that Margaret would be at death's door, but bless you, she's picking up nicely again. She does have her ups and downs, I must say!'

'I think it was really serious,' Barbara protested.

'Well, we can't talk here. I was going home, but let's go for a spin, just for an hour. Come on, what do you say? I'm a good lad at getting you back in time, now aren't I? Admit it?'

And of course, she had to allow that that was true. So she got in, glad to sit down after the long hours of rushing about in Casualty. She was in the act of counting up how many more days she had to serve in that department, and missed what Damien was saying.

He chuckled, patted her hand, and said softly, 'You haven't heard a word! Poor kid, you're tired out. Why don't you have a nap? And do you have to wear that ghastly cap over that glorious hair?'

'Yes, must. I mean, we can't just take off one bit of our uniform — it's full uniform or mufti.'

'Oh well, there it is. Here, have a shoulder to sleep on. It's all right — old Redburn is keeping an eye on us in his mirror!'

And so she dropped off to sleep, and awoke to find they were in Bride's Bay again. 'Well, I did suggest a drink here, now didn't I?' Damien chuckled, turning her distressed face to him. 'It's all right, there's time!'

Somehow it wasn't quite so nice at the Cliff Hotel tonight as it had been on Saturday. Perhaps because she wasn't in the mood, or because she wasn't dressed. The uniform looked out of place, and there was hardly time to enjoy themselves before they had to go again. She didn't know why Damien had brought her, unless it was part of his campaign to establish a habit of taking her out if only for a short while every day.

She promised herself, when they left the hotel that she wouldn't go out with him again. Whatever had attracted her had imperceptibly vanished, and now there was nothing left. She thought of Adam Thorne, and wondered if he would ever be friends with her again, and that left her with a lump in her throat. She was glad when she was back at the hospital.

It was almost lunch-time the next day, when she first became aware that something was wrong. A small enough incident in itself. Two nurses stared at her as they passed; the cold, set stare of curiosity and censure. Barbara had seen it before, when a rumour had built up about some unfortunate girl. It was the same pattern. More and more people stared at her, and their hostility was like a veil, separating her from them.

The rumour itself staggered her more. She caught drifts of it, from different directions, before at last it broke and she was sent for, to go to Matron's office.

It seemed that she had been seen, the night before, in full uniform, furtively leaving the flat where Damien Eldridge was staying!

10

Barbara's chief reaction was amazement, that they should do this to her.

Even Sue was on the side of the rest of them. She had the grace to look ashamed, it was true, when Barbara spoke to her, but as they were just outside Barbara's own room at the time, and no one else was in earshot, Sue had no excuse for not speaking.

'I did warn you, Bar,' she said.

'Look, come into my room. You've changed your apron and I haven't. Now tell me, and frankly, for goodness' sake — what's making people say such a thing about me? I've only been to that flat once, and as I told you, there was a horrid party on. It was so packed that I can't think how they all got in. I certainly didn't go to the flat last night!'

Sue looked flustered, but said nothing.

'I mean it, Sue! That was honestly the only time I ever went there!' Barbara repeated vehemently.

'If you're going to stick to that story, it's okay by me,' Sue said, in a muffled voice. 'But you seem to forget that there was another occasion when you went there, and I heard you arranging to go.'

'When?' Barbara's head shot up in sheer surprise.

'That day — the first day he rang up and asked you over to hear some records. It sounded so fishy that I told him straight off that you wouldn't come! Then when you went on the telephone to him, instead of telling him no yourself, I distinctly heard you say 'All right, I'll come then.' Now you can't deny that, Bar!'

Barbara thought about it, remembering the occasion. Before she could say anything, Sue went on heatedly:

'And when you came off the telephone, I said to you 'You're not going, are you?' or something like that, and that was when you said, 'Yes, why not?' '

'Yes, but that wasn't to the invitation about the records and the flat,' Barbara said, frowning. 'I'd already said no to that, quite definitely. Then he suggested dinner at Bride's Bay, at the Cliff Hotel. I don't know why I agreed to go — to get rid of him, I think. Anyway, it turned out rather nice. It was just that — dinner in a very public place, and afterwards the chauffeur drove us back. All very nice and circumspect!'

Sue stared at her, wanting to believe her. Barbara looked flushed, bothered about something. Sue didn't think she was quite telling the truth.

Barbara was recalling the other painful details about that trip to Bride's Bay. She had been waiting for Adam that night. That was the night she thought he had forgotten all about her, when in fact he had left a note for her and it had miscarried. Saturday night — a mere two nights past — yet it seemed a lifetime away. The doubts and

213

tears of that night had been pushed aside by this new crisis she had been precipitated into.

'I want to believe you,' Sue was saying, 'and I don't know why I can't, except that you're not like you used to be, any more. What I can't understand is why you go out with him at all!'

'I don't *go out with him*!' Barbara said crossly. 'Not in that sense. I mean he isn't a boy-friend, if that's what you mean. I've said this over and over again until I'm tired, but the fact is, I merely went to see him in the first place to try and persuade him to come and see Margaret Knowles — to please Adam Thorne, if you must know!'

'Oh, come off it, Bar — who can you expect to believe that? Well, I mean — Adam Thorne would have asked him himself surely, if he had wanted it that badly!'

'It's too involved to explain,' Barbara said wearily. 'Anyway, you know most of it. You know Damien wanted me to have a screen test — and I only got caught up with that idea because Margaret Knowles kept sending me to his room to ask him things and take the answers back. I wanted my head searching for falling into it! But I hadn't much choice!' she finished, in a bothered voice.

'How do you mean?'

'First of all, Adam Thorne wanted me to take up some things for her. He couldn't get there, and I just happened to be on hand. If only I'd been anywhere else that day!' she fumed. 'But I was helping him. It had to be me — it was Fate, and it's no good kicking against it.'

'Well, that's all right. We all have to fetch and carry at times — no one can help that. But even so, did you have to agree to go out with him, even if he was pressing you to — everyone knows what a flirt Damien Eldridge is! You should have said no and stuck to it, Bar!'

'Adam Thorne took it into his head that it was up to me to get that man to the hospital to see Margaret. I couldn't shift him from the idea that I'd been trying to take Damien from Margaret. He wouldn't budge from the idea!' She was thumping the table with her fist, and she looked more distressed than Sue had even seen her before.

'There you are, you see! He isn't the only one!' Sue pointed out, with good reason. 'You must have done something to make everyone think you were making a play for Damien!'

'But I didn't — all the time I was trying to keep him off, but he said he wouldn't come and see Margaret if I didn't go out with him one evening!'

'That old gag!' Sue scoffed.

'Well, it worked!' Barbara retorted. 'He did come to the hospital, and Margaret was satisfied.'

'All right, but did you have to keep on going out with him? Don't say you didn't — you were seen in his car on Sunday! You were seen getting into his car last night! I just hope you've got some reasonable explanation about last night, if you want people to believe that you didn't go to his flat, that's all!'

'It isn't *his* flat,' Barbara objected, thinking. 'Anyway, it's in a great block of flats, that flat of his friends. Who was it who was supposed to have seen me coming out of No. 27?'

Sue stared. 'I don't know anything about a No. 27,' she said. 'I only know that Weeks and Cartwright were walking back to the bus-stop and they saw you nip out of the main entrance and get into someone's car!'

'Oh, fine,' Barbara said bitterly. 'Staff-nurses, so how can I say they were both seeing double? Just the same, I wasn't near the block of flats. I was at that beastly hotel in Bride's Bay again. We just drove out there for a drink, and back again — and the chauffeur drove us and kept watching us in the mirror! He'll vouch for me!'

'Gosh, look at the time! I shouldn't have stayed here talking all this long! And if I were you, I shouldn't bank on anything the chauffeur might say — everyone will say he's bound to back up his employer, and you can bet Damien won't admit to anything incriminating!'

When Barbara went back on duty, instead of getting a talking-to for being late back from changing her apron, she was sent instead to Matron's Office.

A summons to Matron's Office was the one thing the young nurses dreaded. It hadn't happened to Barbara before, but she knew nurses who had had to report there for misdemeanours. Her heart was pumping madly. Would this be the termination of her nursing career?

A sense of injustice again filled her. So far her time as a nurse at the Hopwood General had been blameless, her work good. She had the name for being an enthusiastic student, and although she didn't know it, her superiors were inclined to add that she was human enough to make the odd mistake, get into the infrequent bout of hot water that made her human. She was well liked, and it was generally recognised that behind that innocent baby-face was a disposition valuable to a nurse because she didn't get in a flap in a crisis. Good nursing material here.

Barbara didn't know all of that. She only knew that she had been very happy and interested and safe, before Margaret Knowles had been admitted to the hospital that day but since Margaret had come into her life, nothing had gone right.

Traditionally, a nurse called up for censure was allowed to cool her heels outside, waiting for the awful summons to come in, but on this occasion, there was no waiting. But before Barbara could raise her hand to tap at the door, it opened and Adam Thorne came out.

He neither looked surprised to see her, nor glad. He gave her the briefest nod, and walked on. Not a word of encouragement, not a hint of what lay in store for her! That treacherous lump came into her throat again, as she raised her hand for the second time to knock, and was at once requested to enter.

She liked Matron. A severe-looking woman behind those heavy horn spectacles, she was fair, just and — in some cases — sympathetic and understanding, so Barbara had heard.

She stood in front of Matron's desk with her hands behind her, her cap pushed well forward, and waited with fast beating heart.

Matron looked thoughtfully at her. 'There has been a rather odd and distressing story brought to me, nurse,' she began, in her forthright way, 'of you being seen coming out of a block of flats, in which one of the patients in the recent road disaster was staying. There seems to be a great deal of significance attaching to this. Perhaps you could explain why.'

It took Barbara completely by surprise, that smooth approach, and nothing in Matron's manner suggested that Barbara was to be suspended. Nonetheless, at the Hopwood General there had been fostered a wariness and respect for authority, which didn't allow her to become unduly optimistic now. She decided on an equally direct approach. 'I believe it was thought that I'd accepted an invitation to go to Damien Eldridge's friends' flat, to be alone with him and listen to records on the player, Matron,' she offered.

'And?'

'He had asked me to, and I'd told him I couldn't. He made a bargain with me to come and see Miss Knowles, if I would go out with him one evening. It was necessary for Miss Knowles to believe that he wanted to visit her, and that he was still going on with his engagement to her, and as that seemed the only way to persuade him to visit her, I agreed — but not to go to the flat or anyone's flat.'

'Did you go out with him, nurse?'

'Yes, Matron, because he kept his part of the bargain and visited the patient.'

'And where do you say you went, if not to the flat from which you were apparently seen coming out by two of our senior nurses?'

Barbara bit her lip. 'The chauffeur drove Mr. Eldridge and me to the Cliff Hotel at Bride's Bay, Matron. I don't know who it was that the two nurses thought they saw coming out of that block, but it wasn't me.'

'I know that,' Matron announced, surprisingly.

Barbara's eyes widened in surprise, but she knew better than to ask how Matron knew it.

Matron didn't keep her in suspense. 'Mr. Thorne has already been to see me. He agrees with me that it wouldn't have been possible for you to be the person at that block of flats, because at that time he himself was looking at you across the restaurant at the Cliff Hotel.'

Barbara's astonishment was clearly unfeigned. 'I didn't see him!' she blurted out.

'I hardly think you did, from what he tells me. He was dining with Miss Whinfield, the aunt of the patient in question. Bride's Bay was a conveniently short distance from her home in Saxonbarn, and although she was rather upset at the time, over her niece, she appears to have been the one who first saw you come into the restaurant, and remembered you as the nurse who had been particularly kind to her one day.' Matron smiled faintly. 'You appear to have two witnesses to your credit, nurse.'

'Yes, Matron. Thank you, Matron,' Barbara murmured, but her head was in a whirl. So that was what he had been to see Matron about! Was it to clear Barbara personally, or was it just that he wasn't going to have damaging rumours flying around, about one of the young nurses in his department (no matter who she was) when he happened to know the rumour was untrue?

'I don't care for rumours, nurse, and I am puzzled to know why this one was started, and how it came about. The nurses are positive it was you — or someone so much like you, even to our uniform — that it was a natural mistake. But I think that hardly likely, though I must say I can't find any other explanation in the circumstances. Have you any enemies, nurse?'

'Enemies!' The idea was new and startling enough to Barbara. 'I don't know of any, Matron. It may have been difficult for other nurses to understand what I was doing, in being seen about with Mr. Eldridge, but I could hardly make my position clear to everyone, without risking it getting back to the patient, and that would have defeated the object. I'm sure she believes she's won Mr. Eldridge back again, although he insists that Miss Knowles is well aware that he doesn't want to marry her now.'

'Yes, Mr. Thorne has explained this tricky position to me, nurse. Well, I must publicly clear up this rumour. I cannot have this sort of thing happening, and I suggest, nurse, that whatever your motives, and however helpful you intended to be, you really must terminate your social engagements with Mr. Eldridge.'

'Yes, Matron!' Barbara agreed heartily.

Thankfully she realised she was dismissed. Never before had she been so glad to get out of a room, nor to feel that she was once again a blameless member of the rest of the nursing staff of the Hopwood General.

There was no opportunity of finding Sue to tell her what had happened and to try to make it up with her, much as Barbara would have liked to. It would be heavenly, she thought to be friends again with Sue, and to talk out of her system the lump of misery and anxiety that had been gathering now for so long. To get back to their old easy friendship together would be a wonderful thing.

She went over to Casualty to report back for duty again and impulsively she went straight to Adam Thorne to thank him. His own nurse looked curiously at her, but said nothing as she went out with a patient, to take her to the X-ray department, leaving Adam alone.

He looked up as Barbara stood beside him.

'I just wanted to thank you. Matron told me,' she said, in a breathless little rush.

He didn't smile, but looked down at the papers he was riffling through. 'I did no more than my duty,' he said repressively.

It was like a slap in the face. She stared at him unbelieving for a moment, then she said, 'Whatever you did it for, I still want to say thank you, because if it hadn't been for what you told Matron, I might have had to leave!'

'You might, indeed,' he agreed gravely, 'but it wasn't I who unwittingly helped you. If Miss Whinfield hadn't spotted you first, I wouldn't have even seen you.'

She flushed angrily. You couldn't have it plainer than that, could you? 'Well, thanks anyway,' she muttered, and went out, biting hard on her bottom lip and mentally kicking herself all the way down Casualty Hall to the pile of dressings waiting to be stacked and sterilised. How big a fool could you get? Why did it have to be Adam Thorne that she had to care so much about? Why couldn't she have taken a header for anyone else on the vast male staff of the hospital? Why did it have to be him, of all people?

She was so angry that she got through far more drums than the other junior working with her, and earned her annoyance. 'You're supposed to be working *with* me, not entering open competition with me!' she snapped.

All the same, the stocking and sterilising was just what Barbara needed just then. A nice even mechanical job that wasn't upsetting, and allowed her to work off her anger and the upsets of that day.

When she had the chance, she went up to see Margaret Knowles. There was no reason to break the habit of looking in on her for a few words, she supposed, just because of all the fuss over Damien Eldridge.

But Margaret wasn't pleased to see her. 'I wonder you had the nerve to come into my room as if nothing had happened!' she said, as Barbara closed the door behind her, and walked over to the bed.

It was only too clear that Margaret had heard the rumour! Barbara bit her lip in vexation. That *would* have to happen! Now everything she had tried to do had been in vain and they were back where they started!

'Would you like me to go?' she asked quietly. There was nothing else she could do.

'No, there are one or two things I want to say to you first!' Margaret said, in a low tense voice. 'You think you're very clever taking Damien from me, but you haven't got him yet! He can have pretty faces for the asking, anywhere, but I've got money, lots of it, and that's what Damien needs most. That's why he needs me!'

'Of course he needs you,' Barbara broke in, 'and for far more important reasons than your money! And believe me, I haven't taken him from you. I wouldn't want to — indeed, it's the last thing I should want to do!'

'I knew you'd deny it,' Margaret told her. 'But you're wasting your time! You can't move in a small place like this without everyone knows what you're doing. It may interest you to know that my aunt saw you with Damien at the Cliff Hotel — she told me so when she came today!'

Barbara sighed. She would have thought that Miss Whinfield would have had more sense. She was such a nice person, but totally without guile. She probably wouldn't understand what Barbara was doing regarding Damien, or what she had hoped to achieve.

'Yes, I know that, but because I was there with him doesn't mean to say that I was taking him from you,' Barbara tried to explain.

She hadn't much hope. Margaret

wasn't in any mood to listen to her, whatever she said.

'You must be mad, to think you can talk me out of believing what I know to be true!' she stormed. 'I knew what sort of person you were, the first time I set eyes on you! I suppose you thought Damien would be easy because you found out he likes girls with your colouring best. I suppose — '

The door clicked, and they both looked up to find Adam Thorne there, looking, Barbara thought wryly, as if he could have knocked both their heads together.

'It appears that I came just in time,' he remarked, on what was for him a very quiet level tone. 'In the first place, Margaret, aren't you being rather silly to get so worked up again? After all we've achieved, surely you should try and help yourself by taking things calmly.'

'Calmly!' she retorted. 'Do you realise what's going on? This — this *person* — ' No words she could think of were scathing enough to describe Barbara, it seemed. 'She's been to the Cliff Hotel at Bride's Bay, with Damien — my Damien — and don't say I'm imagining it, because my aunt told me so!'

'That's quite right,' Adam agreed pleasantly. 'What about it?'

'What d'you mean, Adam? *What about it?*'

'Just that, my dear. What about it? I was there too, remember. I was having dinner with your aunt. I saw them.'

'You saw them? Well, then — '

'Listen, Margaret, my dear,' he said, in a slightly exasperated tone, 'Damien was leaving the hospital, after seeing you, apparently, and seeing Barbara going for a walk, and noticing how tired she looked, he offered her a lift, and very kindly took her out to the coast for a breath of air. Do you mind that?'

'How do you know that? Did she tell you so? Of course she'd make her story good! It wasn't like that at all and you know it! She's taking Damien away from me — '

'Margaret, stop that at once!' His voice wasn't raised much more than a tone or so, but it had the quality of the crack of a whip, and it achieved its object. Margaret quietened at once, and lay looking up at him.

'Now then, let's have this quite clear, my dear. I know you've had a very rough time, and you've had a major operation, but you're getting over it, and it doesn't mean that you can demand limitless things from everyone around you.'

'What d'you mean, Adam?' Margaret gasped.

'Be reasonable, my dear! I'd broken one date with Barbara to stay with you the night after your operation, because your aunt couldn't be here. Your aunt was distressed and anxious last night so I took her to dinner, when I might have been out with Barbara. Now, are you going to begrudge Damien giving Barbara a breath of air as well?'

'*You* taking her out?' Margaret asked blankly, and looked from one to the other of them. 'You're just saying that! Why should you be dating *her?*'

Adam's lips set in a firm line which Barbara knew well. He looked as if he would have liked to shake Margaret, but instead, to the surprise of both of them, he said, quite quietly, 'For the usual reason, Margaret, my dear. We're going to be engaged, Barbara and I!'

11

It was difficult to decide who looked more astonished — Margaret, or Barbara herself!

And then Adam's hand was on Barbara's shoulder, pressing firmly, signalling (it seemed to Barbara) a warning to act naturally, as if that announcement of his were indeed the truth.

She was in a turmoil, and the pressure of his hand on her shoulder did little to ease the excitement in her. He must surely feel how her blood was racing through her veins and how she was trembling all over.

Margaret was no less excited, but in her case it took a different form. It meant that this girl wasn't interested in her Damien at all, if she were going to be engaged to Adam! As Margaret knew well, Adam wasn't the man to share any girl-friend of his, and he had already lost one to Damien Eldridge.

Her face lit up. 'Oh, I'm so glad — so glad for you both!' she exclaimed, holding out the one hand that had now had its bandage removed. It was the left hand, but it was no less hearty in the way it grasped first Adam's and then Barbara's, than if it had been her right hand. 'I had no idea! How long has this been going on? Have you been on the point of an engagement all the time I've been in hospital, and you never even hinted to me, Adam? For shame — an old friend like me! You should have told me!'

'You weren't in any condition to listen to my private affairs,' Adam said mildly.

But he looked at Margaret, and waited, and rather belatedly she took the hint and turned to Barbara.

'I suppose you think I'm rather awful, saying all those things to you about Damien,' she began, smiling. 'But what else could I think? Everyone was talking about it, and lying here helpless, there was nothing else I could do but believe it. After all, I don't know you very well. For all I know, you might be one of those people who make a habit of snatching other people's men. Damien's terribly good-looking and well-known, and lots of girls would give their ears to get him!'

And that, Barbara saw, was as far as Margaret would ever get towards saying she was sorry.

'It's all right,' she said. 'So long as you do really understand now!'

But Margaret had turned back to Adam. Clearly she had no use for Barbara or any other girl, for that matter. She was a young woman who liked men and got on well with them. Only with men could she be bothered to exert herself to be pleasant.

'Oh, Adam darling, I am glad you've got fixed up again — I've been so worried about you!'

Adam took that with a pinch of salt.

'Yes, but don't tell anyone,' he remembered to warn her. 'You are the only one to be told so far, and that's only because you needed to be convinced that Barbara isn't interested in your fiancé.'

Margaret looked doubtful. 'She doesn't look very happy about it. Neither do you, come to think of it. I suppose it is true? Then why is it being kept a secret?'

'Well, you know how it is in hospital,' Adam said. 'We don't want to be teased — we don't want to talk about it at all just yet.'

'When are you going to buy the ring?' Margaret persisted.

'We haven't even got round to discussing it yet, but when we do, we'll come straight along to show it to you.'

Barbara got up. 'I really ought to go,' she said. She had had enough of this difficult business, and she badly wanted to get Adam alone to ask him why he had gone to such lengths, and how he thought they were going to get out of it.

To announce an engagement was the last thing she had expected of him, even if the position had appeared very difficult for the moment.

Adam said, 'Oh, yes, look at the time! Must dash now, Margaret, but one or the other of us will be looking in later. 'Bye for now, my dear!'

'Goodbye,' Margaret said slowly, and there was a very thoughtful look on her face.

When her nurse came in presently, she said carelessly, 'Have you heard the rumour that's going around about that Nurse Caley?' To Margaret, this was no worse than the average white lie. She often said the wrong to get the right. It was just a case of being clever, tripping the other person into disclosing what she knew.

In this case she succeeded completely. Her nurse spun round. 'Now how on earth did you hear about that? It's all being hushed up!'

'What on earth for? Or is it true, then?' Margaret asked, frowning. Why,

she asked herself, should that engagement be 'hushed up' or was the nurse
talking about something else?

'Well, if you've already heard the
rumour, and you don't mind, I suppose
there's no harm in discussing it. You
see, although those two seniors say they
saw her coming out of that block of
flats, in uniform too, the Casualty
Officer said he saw her in quite a
different place at the same time. Your
aunt was with him and said so, too, so
of course, it's difficult to know just
what to believe.'

'Yes, my aunt told me she'd seen her
in Bride's Bay,' Margaret said quickly,
glad to be able to contribute something.
But she was thinking fast. What flat?
What had been going on that they
hadn't told her about? And had the
nurses really seen Barbara Caley,
perhaps made a mistake in the time?
Could it be that Adam had merely said
quickly that he was engaged to Barbara,
to get her out of a hole?

The nurse was looking curiously at

her. 'You must be feeling a lot better, not to mind your fiancé being coupled with a rumour like this!' she remarked, busily dusting and tidying. 'Personally I think it's just a bit of malicious gossip, though I can't think what's at the back of it. Everyone likes Caley. She's a nice little thing, the last one to have a man ask her round to his place all alone to listen to records. That's too much an 'oldie' to be tried out, surely? Though I don't know — Caley does look rather young and innocent, and people might think it worth a try, and the trouble is, word got around that he asked her on the hospital phone — a friend of hers took the message. Oh, no, it can't be true!'

'No, I don't think it's true,' Margaret said softly, rage and jealousy warring in her half-closed eyes. So that's what had been going on, and that girl had sat beside her protesting that there was nothing between her and Damien! Well, there was something Margaret could do to make things difficult for her. For

Adam, too, to punish him for protecting that girl! So they wanted to keep their engagement secret, did they? Well, let's see what this will do, Margaret thought.

'No, it can't be true,' she added, thinking. 'Because I've heard (but keep it dark, won't you?) that she and the Casualty Officer are secretly engaged.'

The nurse, who loved a bit of gossip, almost dropped the vase of flowers she was holding, in sheer surprise. 'Did you say the Casualty Officer? Oh, no, surely not — he's supposed to be a woman-hater since — oh!' She realised, too late, that the patient had been having a game with her, leading her skilfully into deep waters, and that this, too, was the girl who had been engaged to Adam Thorne, and had caused him to earn the reputation of being a woman-hater.

But why, why in the name of wonder, did Margaret Knowles introduce the subject in the first place? Or didn't she mind, now that she was engaged to the film star?

Deeply embarrassed, the nurse made good her escape, intent only on finding out from someone how much truth there was in that rumour the patient had introduced herself.

At the end of the corridor was a small room, used for putting the vases of flowers in, at night. As she passed, the nurse caught sight of Barbara in there. She pushed the door open a little. 'I say, Caley, have you heard — ' she began, when the door opened wider, and she saw that there was someone with Barbara: the Casualty Officer himself.

Her confusion complete now, the nurse backed out with a muttered apology. What were they doing behind the half-closed door of the flower-room, she asked herself furiously? And Caley had looked anything but her usual calm self! So it must be true! They must be engaged!

She sped on down the corridor, intent only on finding someone else to talk it over with.

But for Barbara, that was the worst thing that could have happened. 'It's all very well for you to cook up that story on the spur of the moment, Mr. Thorne, but where's it going to lead to? I don't think the patient even believed it, but you saw her nurse look in just now! You know what that means! If she hasn't already heard it from Miss Knowles, she'll make a guess and something will start and it'll be all over the hospital in no time!'

'You're imagining things,' he said testily. 'All I wanted to do was to shock Margaret into believing that there was nothing between you and Eldridge. I hope it's true, that's all! You haven't reassured me on that point.'

'What else can I do but tell you, again and again, that I am not trying to take him from her. Really, it isn't fair! I wouldn't have known him in the first place if she hadn't kept sending me over to talk to him, and then you wanted me to arrange for him to visit her. I wish I'd refused to help you both.

Now look at the mess I'm in!'

'Is it such a mess?' he asked, after a minute. 'Do you think it would be too much to ask, to pretend to be engaged to me for a little while, until Margaret is well enough to leave the hospital?'

'For a little while! Does that mean you'd be willing to break the engagement then?'

'If I say it's temporary, then it is!'

'I should have thought you'd have had enough of broken engagements!' she retorted, impulsively. Then she saw how her hasty words had affected him. 'I'm sorry. That wasn't nice of me. I didn't mean to hurt you, but I'm so tired of all this!'

'Bear with it for a little while longer,' he said, softly. 'Once Margaret's out of the hospital it will all be over and you'll be as you were again!'

As she walked down the corridor, back to Casualty, Barbara thought that he had never been more wrong. She had been engaged to him — even if it were only a pretence in the preposterous effort to please this difficult patient — and life for Barbara could never ever be the same again.

In the next twenty-four hours, however, several things happened to change their immediate plans. The first thing was that Margaret's nurse had spread the rumour all over the hospital in her effort to discover whether it was indeed the truth. The hospital was agog with the news! That the Casualty Officer had become engaged to Nurse Caley, on top of the rumour that Nurse Caley had spent the evening alone with the film star, leaving the flat in a furtive manner — these were goings on to brighten the most mundane routine at the Hopwood General.

Then, too, Matron had to be smoothed down. Her feathers were badly ruffled to think that during her careful and generous handling of that rumour, she hadn't been told of Barbara's engagement to the Casualty Officer. Adam again had to exercise his charm over Matron, but in doing so, he was admitting to the whole hospital that it was true. He was engaged to be married again, after that broken engagement not much more than a year ago, and to the patient, at that!

Then, too, so many people appeared to be hurt because they hadn't been let into the secret. Sue, for one. Barbara had a very difficult time with her.

'Sue, I didn't know myself until all of a sudden. It's . . . it's just one of those things, I suppose!'

'But I thought you didn't even like him!' Sue objected.

'What is more to the point, I didn't think he liked me,' Barbara offered, and although that was in part the truth, it was at the same time a twisting of the truth to suit the occasion, a fact which bothered her so much that it spoilt even the little pleasure she was getting out of this sham romance. And she had to admit that she was getting pleasure out of even the slightest connection with Adam Thorne.

People now smiled at her in approval, where not so many hours back they were lifting their eyebrows, cold hostility and frowning disapproval in their faces.

'How long has this been going on, Bar?'

'You're a dark horse, Bar — we thought you were such a quiet little thing!'

'Has he bought a ring?'

'What's he like, Bar — isn't it awkward, with *her* in hospital? You know all about that old affair, don't you, Bar?' And so it went on. Enquiries meant to be kindly.

Margaret's aunt was hurt, too, that Adam hadn't told her. She considered he must have known, that evening at the hotel in Bride's Bay, and she felt that he might have hinted to her the true state of affairs.

He hadn't the heart to tell her that she didn't even know when she was letting a secret out, and that this hadn't been meant to get around.

And, of course, Damien Eldridge didn't like it, either. Margaret had a great deal of pleasure in telling him about it when he visited her, and of wanting to know the truth about the earlier rumour.

'Honestly, Margaret, I don't know what you're talking about! Of course Barbara didn't come to the flat at night to be alone with me! She's such a frightened little mouse, it's a wonder she dares to be seen out with a chap in broad daylight! Who started this nonsense, anyway?'

'I don't know, and I'd like to know,' Margaret said softly. 'You see, someone was seen, someone like that girl — enough like her to convince not one nurse, but two! Senior nurses, at that! And the uniform of this hospital was used.'

The way she said it set him thinking. If she had said that it was a nurse in the hospital's uniform, he might not have taken any notice. But the phrasing was peculiar.

It nagged at him so much that he didn't take in half of what Margaret was saying about Barbara becoming engaged to Adam Thorne. 'She's really engaged to him!' she said, and Damien realised that she wasn't really pleased. Margaret was bitterly jealous of Barbara.

'Don't be silly, Margaret, it's just one of those silly rumours. Of course she isn't engaged to the chap. She isn't engaged to anyone!'

'But she is! They wanted to keep it secret, but I — well, I just happened to mention it to my nurse, just to see if she'd heard the rumour or not. Well, she was absolutely knocked over with the news. She of course promptly spread it around, although she knew it was supposed to be kept dark, and there it is! All over the hospital and they haven't denied it! So it must be true! Adam, whom I might have married myself!'

'You still had the chance,' Damien pointed out angrily. 'He's been dancing attendance on you ever since you came into hospital.'

He was fuming about the news, now that it had sunk into his head that it might possibly be true. To think Barbara had succeeded in persuading him to keep visiting Margaret, leading him to think that she would do anything in return, and all the time she was getting secretly engaged to the Casualty Officer. Well, if she thought she could make a fool of Damien Eldridge, she was wrong. If anyone threw anyone over, it was Damien, not a little nurse at some small-town hospital in which they had got caught up.

His desire for her still gnawed at him, but now it was entangled with his anger at what he termed Barbara's duplicity and his main desire was to hurt her.

Adam, too, was very angry. That news should never have leaked out, but Margaret, he knew, was a law unto herself. If she felt like telling anyone, she would.

He asked her about it, after Damien had left her room. Margaret was prettily sorry, and admitted she had started it.

'It's your own fault, Adam! You gave me the odd feeling that you were making it all up, so I just asked my nurse if she'd heard anything about it. That's all! But the silly girl caught on to the idea and must have rushed around telling everyone it had really happened. So you see, it's no use blaming me. Why don't you want people to know about it — or isn't it the real thing? Now I wonder why you should tell me she's engaged to you if it isn't so?'

'Never mind, Margaret,' he said wearily, 'It's all over the place and nothing can be done about it. Meantime, I have some good news for you. There's a chap coming to see you about some further treatment. He's an excellent surgeon, a charming fellow, and I want you to be as co-operative as you can. I really believe we shall have you up and about long before we thought we should.'

'How you wrap it all up!' she said softly, her eyes unforgiving in spite of her smiling mouth. 'I've seen my face. Oh, I know you left instructions, and so did the rest of them, that I shouldn't see a mirror. Why do you suppose I collapsed the day that Damien went home? Because I was filled with grief and shock, on account of his not coming to see me? No, no, no! Do you think I don't know that that conceited little brute doesn't want me any more?'

Adam's jaw dropped. 'Did you know?'

'Of course I did! And do you think, now you've somehow managed to get him to come here and pretend he loves me, do you really think I'm fool enough not to see how he flinches when he looks at me? What a complete blind idiot you must all take me for!'

'But how did you — ?' he began desperately.

'I saw my reflection in a polished metal bowl, on the dressing trolley when the nurse's back was turned for a minute. You never thought of that possibility, did you?'

He said something under his breath. He looked very put out indeed.

'That, my dear Adam, was enough to upset anyone. But it had its amusing side, watching you all rushing round in a flat spin, thinking I was crying for Damien, trying to persuade him to come to the hospital. I've got news for you, Adam my sweet. I wouldn't marry Damien Eldridge now, if he came to me on bended knees. *And* I'm going to withdraw my money. You have no idea how much he's persuaded my aunt — and me — to part with, for one thing and another.'

'I can't believe all this is true, Margaret,' Adam said, in a distressed voice. 'I can't believe you're not going on with him. I can't believe you'd call in any money you'd lent him and what's more, I can't believe you've lent all that much to anyone in the first place. Oh, I know you and your aunt have a great deal of assets between you, but from my recollection, neither of you parted with them.'

She smiled without rancour. Adam was much too old a friend to quarrel with. 'Just the same, it's been rather amusing.'

He strode up and down. 'Amusing! My heavens!' he muttered, and she watched him with speculation now.

'Are there some things you've done to help me which you wouldn't have done, if you'd known the truth?' she asked softly.

She almost caught him unawares. He almost blurted out that neither he nor Barbara would have wasted any time over Damien Eldridge if they'd known. He stopped just in time. Not only because he wasn't intending to let Margaret know that, but in Barbara's case he wasn't really sure that that was true. Just how much did she really like that fellow? If she had known the truth, would she have striven so hard to persuade him to come and see Margaret? Might she not have pursued a different course? Adam couldn't be sure in his heart that Barbara was as unattracted to Eldridge as she had protested.

'Well,' he said briskly, 'if you know about your face, that certainly simplifies our position. Instead of waiting for a problematical right moment to break it to you, we can now forge ahead without fearing the consequences.'

'Forge ahead?' she asked, warily.

'With plastic surgery — or were you expecting to stay in that interesting condition for always, Margaret, so that you could have yet another weapon with which to torture those near and dear to you?'

'I suppose you don't still love me?' she murmured, smiling a little.

He saw in that moment, that she was hoping he would give a sign that that was so. He stood looking down at her for a moment, thinking what sort of a life would stretch ahead of him, if he did still love her and she found out. She would never give him any peace.

He drew a deep breath and prepared to tell her something that even Barbara didn't know, and he was relieved that he could tell Margaret, and that it was the truth. 'No, I've got over you. It's Barbara now.'

Just putting it into words seemed to make it more possible, although he thought he knew in his heart that Barbara could never care for anyone else after having been dazzled by Eldridge.

Nonetheless, he went to find Barbara. She was bandaging a child's forearm, telling him something that made him chuckle and forget his discomfort, and there was a warm, glorious smile on that young smooth face of hers. He wanted to take her into his arms and kiss her. After all, he had some sort of right to now, surely?

It tore at him to see the way that smile faded when she turned to find him standing there looking at her.

'Did you want me, Mr. Thorne? I've finished here now,' she said, uncertainly.

He nodded, and waited while she returned the little boy to his mother.

When Barbara returned, he said formally, 'I'm afraid it's all over the hospital, so I think for our own sakes we'd better act naturally, don't you?'

She was alarmed at the way her pulses leaped and raced.

'What d'you mean, Mr. Thorne?'

'Nothing very dreadful,' he hastily reassured her. 'Just the obvious thing — a date together. Tonight. That elusive date that we didn't seem to manage, will do.'

12

'Where would you like to go?' Adam murmured, as he drove Barbara away from the hospital that evening.

'I don't mind,' she said, at a loss. He hadn't asked her where she would like to go, on that other occasion when he had taken her to the hotel for coffee, but now she sensed that it was all different. She had meantime been out frequently with Damien Eldridge. Adam was subtly indicating that he had lost touch with her; that she may have had her tastes changed, indeed been changed herself by Damien's alien influence.

'No. I suppose it isn't important,' he sighed. 'Well, you won't want the Cliff Hotel in Bride's Bay again, I'm sure! We'd better decide on something simple. There's a place outside Maplefield that might do.'

She flushed. It was going to be that sort of evening! He was going to make her feel rather guilty about her dates with Damien. Obviously he thought that there had been other ways in which to persuade Damien that his duty lay with the patient, other than letting him take her out to expensive places in the full public eye!

All this didn't make for a nice easy atmosphere between them, which was a pity, because the little place he had mentioned outside Maplefield turned out to be rather pleasing.

It was one of the last sixteenth century properties left in the district, and it had been bought by an Army colonel after he had had an accident which had left him permanently lame.

'One of my patients,' Adam said, before he introduced Barbara.

Colonel Rand was a nice man. Pleasantly ugly, with a bristling ginger moustache and hair to match. In his late forties, and still very vigorous in spite of his limp, he was plainly quite delighted to hear that Adam was again contemplating matrimony.

It smote Barbara, for to her the whole thing was no more than a wicked farce, and as such it ought to have been kept a secret.

She said as much when the Colonel left them alone at a secluded table, after toasting their future at the private bar in his own den.

'Oh, I don't know!' Adam said, one eyebrow lifted in what Barbara considered was nothing more nor less than blatant amusement. 'Since Margaret has ensured that everyone in the hospital knows, why should I keep it from a very old friend of mine? What's the matter? Didn't you like Colonel Rand?'

'Yes, I did! I liked him too much to enjoy seeing him be duped by this — this idiotic arrangement! If you had to tell him, why didn't you say it was just — just — '

'Oh, come now, I hardly see myself telling an old friend that I've been jockeyed into this awkward position by the very person who jilted me not so many months ago. Can you?'

'You're bitter, rather than hurt!' Barbara marvelled.

'I don't like to be made a fool of, any more than the next fellow,' he agreed, watching her. 'I'm sorry you look on all this as just a farce, too!'

'Well, what do you look on it as?'

'As a temporary engagement,' he said carefully. 'One that you might grow so used to, that — well, even if you wouldn't consider a permanent engagement, you might come to feel that it isn't so bad. And believe me, it might drag on for some time, knowing Margaret! Much as she seems to want to marry Eldridge, she won't rush into it until her face has been put right.'

'How long will that be?'

'Who knows? Certainly some time!'

'You said we only had to go on with this engagement until she left the Hopwood General! She won't have the plastic surgery done here, will she?'

'I hardly think so, but she has to have one more operation before she can leave here. She's seeing the surgeon about it tomorrow.'

'Who's going to do it?' Barbara asked, trying to keep her mind on hospital affairs rather than to take notice of the way her hand was shaking when he passed the menu to her.

'Gifford Donahue. Only the best for Margaret.'

'Oh, that nice man! I saw him once, during my first week out of P.T.S. I was so scared. Believe it or not, I'd got lost, trying to find the path. lab. I was rushing around with a blood sample. He stopped. He looked down at me so kindly. I remember, his hair was almost white, yet he had a young face and terribly blue eyes. And he said something about me looking so pale that I needed some blood! I nearly burst into tears on the spot.'

'What happened?' Adam asked gently, picturing that frightened young girl, who didn't look very much older now, facing him across the table. This was the girl that the world thought he was going to marry. He wished fervently that it were true. 'He didn't let you go with a joke, I know!'

'No, you're right. He took me there himself. Said it was all on his way, but I don't believe it. And he said a few things. I don't remember what they were. I only know they made me feel less of a nitwit everyone despised. I'll never forget him.'

'How would you like to meet him again — as my fiancée — or would that be too painful?'

She was mercifully saved from answering that, by the arrival of the waiter. He brought a bucket of ice, with an imposing bottle lying in it, which he proceded to open. She noticed, then, that there were tall stemmed shallow bowled glasses. She shot a startled glance at Adam, and her lips framed the word: 'Champagne?' and her eyebrows rose interrogatively.

He nodded, with a faint smile. The

waiter left them and Adam said, 'Why not champagne? It's usual in the circumstances, isn't it?'

She raised her own glass to her lips, for the sake of something to do, so that he shouldn't see them trembling. What a wicked thing it was that she had to go through this, knowing it wasn't true, when at this stage — this late stage — it was borne in on her that here was the one man she would have liked to spend her life with!

'You'll be producing an engagement ring next,' she said shakily, putting her glass down, and making a valiant attempt to laugh.

'I thought of that, too,' Adam said, and searched in his pocket.

'Oh, no! No, don't do that!' she protested.

'Why not? As you say, it's the normal thing to follow the champagne with!'

'Please, isn't it enough to pretend so hard and to deceive nice people like the colonel? Don't go so far as to give me a ring. I couldn't bear it!'

'A ring can always be returned,' he said, the harsh note creeping into his voice again.

She had reminded him of that first time, she thought, contrition flooding her. Why didn't she let him do as he wanted to? If it was so important to play-act like this, why couldn't she do her share? It wasn't as if there were anyone else in her life who mattered all that much! If he could do it, hurting himself by repeating the performance, surely she could pull her weight?

And so, when he opened the box, she obediently put her left hand forward. 'All right, then,' she murmured.

He hesitated. 'That isn't the one which I gave Margaret,' he told her, with rare perception, and was rewarded by her face clearing. 'Did you think I'd give you the same ring?'

'Oh, then that's all right!' she said, and even managed a smile, though her eyes were too bright. He didn't know that she had assumed that this, therefore, was a cheap ring, bought for the occasion, and that it consequently didn't matter.

For Barbara, that put the whole thing in its right perspective. Play-acting, with a ring that was no more than a 'prop'; a ring too new and cheap to have any special memories or significance.

He slid it on to her finger. It almost fitted. Her hand, he reflected, was the same type as his grandmother's; small, beautifully shaped, and considering the work a nurse had to do, it was beautifully kept, and the skin wasn't red and chafed. A nice little hand, one that his grandmother would have approved of, to wear her ring.

Colonel Rand went by, and paused to admire it. 'Oh, delightful!' he said. 'If I'm not mistaken, that's — '

He broke off as Adam shook his head warningly at him. Barbara hadn't seen that bit of by-play. She had been looking up at Adam's friend.

'That's what?' she asked him.

The Colonel recovered himself very

quickly, considering he had been about to remark that the last time he had seen that ring, it had been in the Thorne collection, on show for some charity, among the late Lady Amelia's other treasures. Instead, he finished smoothly, ' — almost a perfect fit, which is pretty good guesswork on the part of the future bridegroom!' and bowing slightly he hurried away smiling.

'You like it then?' Adam said quickly, before Barbara had a chance to question him.

'Oh, yes, it's very pretty, and I'm glad you got it. It will make it more convincing for Miss Knowles, when she demands to see it — as she will, of course!'

'Yes, well, perhaps you'd better not show her, on second thoughts. Tell her you aren't allowed to wear it, on duty.'

'All right, if you say so,' Barbara agreed doubtfully.

'Haven't you — do you know much about stones?' he asked, puzzled. It was clear that she didn't realise the value of that ring, and he hoped she wouldn't think it of so little value that she could be careless with it and lose it. At the same time, it wouldn't do to let Barbara know it's real worth, feeling as she did about this engagement.

Besides, there was the question of Margaret, who had wanted his mother's ring, because it was the only one she had seen. If she knew that this girl had got Adam's grandmother's ring, a collection piece, there would really be sparks flying!

Yet he wanted Barbara to have it. The way he felt at the moment, he would have given her the moon, if it had been his to give.

Especially at this moment, the way she was looking at him. 'Don't be silly,' she said, genuinely amused. 'I've never had any jewellery at all, ever. Oh, the odd cheap necklace I've bought myself, since I've been working, but never before. Orphans don't, you know. Not usually.'

'Oh, my dear, I'm sorry. I didn't know!'

'It's all right! I don't mind anyone knowing. I lived with the usual elderly aunt. She was very hard up but even if she hadn't been, she wouldn't have let me wear jewellery. She didn't believe in it.'

'Tell me about it.'

'I will if you promise not to be sorry for me. She was rather a dear, in her austere way. She never asked me to put up with something she wouldn't put up with herself. What she had, she shared. I had enough to eat. We lived in an old-fashioned house that was comfortable without being smart. And when she died, it reverted to the estate of her own mother who had left it for her to live in during her life-time.'

'So there was nothing for you?'

'No, but luckily I was just old enough to start being a nurse, so I came straight to the hospital. It's been fun. Lots of other young people my age.

Never a dull moment — never an idle moment. That was what I'd feared most. I'd been brought up to be afraid of idleness, you see.'

'Yes, but didn't you want the same things other young people had?'

'Not really. What you never have, you never miss.' She smiled. 'What else could I want for — I wanted to nurse, and I've got it.'

'I see now why Eldridge fascinated you so much,' he murmured, half to himself. 'Meeting someone you've known on the screen — yes, who could blame you for having your head turned by all that glitter and glamour?'

'I did want to see what it was like,' she allowed, 'but when I did see, I didn't like it much. It was so very noisy,' she added.

'You must think this very dull,' he said, frowning. 'But this is my kind of background. This is what I like. I should have thought! You'd have preferred to dance!'

She didn't argue with him. If that

was what he thought she was like, there was no point in denying it, letting him think she was being agreeable and not meaning it. He wouldn't believe that she had dreamed of coming to one of these old places, where the flagstones dipped drunkenly towards the walls, with age, and the beams were genuinely blackened. This must have been a private house once; guns and trophies were hung in embrasures in the walls, and each end of the room had an enormous fireplace, where logs were supported by ancient dogs, and threw a cheerful glow.

This was the real thing; not the fake, which was what she would get with someone like Damien Eldridge. But she couldn't expect Adam Thorne to believe that.

'Come on, let's go. We'll find somewhere gay.'

She let him terminate the evening at this quiet, restful place, because she was out of her depth now.

He took her into Maplefield, to the

largest hotel, where there was dancing, bright lights, a very good band, and all the things that he thought she would like.

But when they were on the dance floor, his arms around her, she wished with all her heart that she had had the sense to prevent this. She should have known how his touch would have an upsetting effect on her. It was bad enough when he put a friendly hand beneath her elbow to help her up the steps coming in, but now — close to him, caught in the swaying mass of people in the middle of the floor, she felt so shaken that her legs were weak and wobbly.

'What's the matter? Cold?' he asked, aware that her hand was trembling in his.

'No, nothing,' she said, in a muffled voice.

He, too, was shaken, but he felt he owed this part of the evening to her, poor child. She had certainly had the worst of this business with Margaret.

Their steps matched perfectly, although she was so small and slight. It should have been a wonderful experience, she told herself fiercely, but after a while she felt she couldn't stand any more of it. It wasn't fair that she had been manoeuvred into this position, feeling as she did about him! But it was essential that she shouldn't let him know, and, if she stayed here any longer, he would surely find out for himself what an effect he was having on her.

'I'm rather tired,' she said at last. 'Could we go back, Mr. Thorne?'

'You'd better get used to saying Adam,' he told her.

'*Adam*,' she whispered, obediently, but the uttering of his name almost finished her.

'Let's go,' he said shortly.

They threaded their way through the dancers. She got her coat while he brought the car round. Not long now, she told herself, before I'm back at the Home, and I promise myself I won't be let in for this sort of evening again!

The ring on her finger mocked her. Of course she would have to go out with him again, all the while she had that!

He drove back in grim silence, but she was used to that, and thought nothing of it, until she saw, with surprise, that he was not pulling up in the usual place, but driving openly into the main gate of the Nurses' Home.

'We're engaged, remember?' he said softly, as he helped her out. 'And engaged people have to say a proper goodnight.'

She heard people walking up the path. Other nurses returning. Obediently she put her face up for a brief kiss, before escaping.

It started as a brief kiss, but with the touch of her lips on his, it was as if a flame shot up between them. Standing there in the darkness, between the car and the dense bank of laurels, Barbara forgot that this was in the hospital grounds, five minutes from her safe little room in the Home, to which she had been making as for sanctuary.

She clung to him as he clung to her, all sense of time gone. Then he put her gently from him.

'Better go in, now,' he whispered huskily. 'Goodnight, my dearest,' and he gave her a gentle push towards the front door.

Her heart was still banging fit to suffocate her, and she walked unsteadily in. She heard the car door slam and was aware of him driving away, past the Home, to the Residents' Car Park. Two other nurses passed her.

'Hi, Bar!' they called. 'We just heard — congratulations!'

That was echoed, everywhere she went, in varying ways, but she hardly noticed. All she could see was his white face, as he put her from him, after that kiss. All she could ask herself was: Was it really only for the benefit of other people who might pass and see them? Was it?

13

Barbara didn't know what she expected, the next day on duty. She went to Casualty with mixed feelings, but she was surprised to find Adam Thorne the same in his manner as he had always been. A cool little smile that might appear correct to everyone else, but to Barbara — who knew the truth behind this engagement — it suggested that he was sorry for his ardour of the night before, and wished to forget it.

She grew hot all over as she remembered that kiss. She asked herself for the hundredth time what had made him do it. He had made everything else painfully clear about this strange engagement, and then, at the last moment, he had kissed her as if he really cared for her!

The ring Adam had given her was now hanging on the chain she wore under her uniform; the chain holding her late aunt's modest little ring — the one thing the old lady had left her — and it occurred to Barbara that the new ring was much heavier. Compared with her aunt's ring, the setting was altogether different, the stones winked in the light, and their depths had blue fire, making the one stone in her aunt's ring look no more than a chip of glass.

The comparison made Barbara feel vaguely uneasy. She decided to show Sue the ring Adam had given her, and see what her reactions were. But Sue, of course, would naturally expect a fine ring from someone like Adam Thorne. If Barbara allowed her doubts about it to show, that would surely make Sue begin to be suspicious, which was the last thing Barbara wanted.

Sue came to sit by her at lunch and promptly gave Barbara something else to be anxious about. 'I say, everyone's talking about your engagement, so it didn't matter about Damien Eldridge knowing, did it?'

In the upheaval of her engagement to Adam Thorne, Barbara had forgotten this aspect. 'Have you spoken to him, then, Sue?'

'Um, he telephoned. Couldn't find you. I was in a hurry, anyway, so I just gave him the bare details. Well, he can hardly expect to keep dating you now, can he?'

'What did he say?'

'He was a bit peculiar, frankly. He couldn't take it in at first, and then he sounded so furious, he could hardly speak. I say, it *is* all right — him knowing — isn't it?'

'Well, yes, I suppose so. It was meant to be kept a secret, but it got out, so — oh, I don't know!'

'You can sort it out when he comes to see his dear Margaret this afternoon. He said he's coming,' Sue finished. 'Has Adam Thorne given you a ring yet?'

'Yes. I'll show you later, but not here. I don't want anyone else to see it just yet,' Barbara murmured.

278

'Okay, when we go up to change our aprons, eh?' Sue said. She was clearly thrilled about this. Damien Eldridge had had his day, while he had been in the hospital. Excitement is transient in a place where everyone lives on excitement. He was no longer a patient. Today the rage of the hospital was the astounding engagement of the Casualty Officer to the pretty little nurse who had been helping him.

Damien himself realised the change in the atmosphere when he arrived that afternoon to see Margaret. Nurses no longer stared at him. They were used to the sight of a film star about the place.

His visit to Margaret wasn't a success, either. 'Well, darling,' she began, 'your little friend has got herself engaged to Adam. Have you heard?'

'Have I heard!' he said savagely. 'Can't anyone talk about anything else in this place? Why should I care what she does, anyway?'

'Oh, don't you? Then I'm glad, darling. I thought you were rather interested in her. Are you sure you haven't invited her to have a screen test?'

'You know I wouldn't do that, Margaret!'

'On the contrary,' she drawled, 'I'm pretty sure you would!'

She was perverse, irritating, tantalising, as only Margaret knew how to be, and Damien was glad when he could at last decently get up and leave her.

All he wanted was to find Barbara, discover what this nonsense was all about. He couldn't believe that without letting him know a thing about it, she would quietly get engaged to some other man. She couldn't do that to him!

The fact that he was engaged to Margaret, meant nothing to him. He wanted Barbara so badly that he hadn't thought about Margaret at all, unless it was to believe that Margaret was so anxious to keep his love that she would shut her eyes to any little amorous adventures he might have with young nurses in the hospital.

He surprised Barbara just leaving the Home after changing her apron, and showing her ring to the astonished Sue, who could only repeat, 'It's fabulous, Bar — fabulous!'

'Barbara!' Damien said urgently. 'I must talk to you!'

'Not now, Damien! Not here, in full view of everyone — you'll get me into trouble!'

'When can I talk to you then?' he insisted.

'I'll let you know,' she said, nervously, one eye on the time. 'No, you must let me go — I've been too long already!' and she flew down the path back to the hospital.

He knew it was no use bothering her now, so he decided to wait in the car tonight when she came off duty.

Barbara, however, was standing in for another nurse who had gone sick. Casualty was very busy that day and the hours were changed in many cases. Barbara came off duty earlier, but

Damien didn't know that.

She wondered uneasily if Damien would try to contact her. She felt instinctively that he wouldn't let the matter rest there. He had indicated all along that he was only waiting for the chance to terminate his engagement to Margaret, before turning to Barbara. He wouldn't be pleased with the news that Barbara had all the time been thinking of someone else, Adam Thorne of all people!

She hoped Adam would suggest spending at least part of the evening with her, but he was at the end of the hall talking to the Superintendent, and he walked off with him.

Barbara felt deeply disappointed. She told herself sharply that Adam hadn't known that that would happen. Well, she wasn't doing anything that evening, and he knew where to find her if he wanted her.

She hurried across to the Nurses' Home, intent on finding Sue, but she had gone out for an unexpected trip into Larksgate with Colin Price, Barbara heard.

It looked like an evening that might well be spent on mugging up her neglected notes, she told herself firmly, but she had hardly started on them when she was called to the telephone. 'Yes, Barbara Caley speaking,' she said.

'I've been asked to give you a message,' a woman's voice at the other end said. 'Will you go at once to the bus stop at Church Corner on the Ring Road and wait to be picked up in the car?'

'Who asked you to give me this message?' Barbara said, half afraid that it might be Damien.

'Well, he said he didn't want any names mentioned and that you'd understand why,' the woman said.

That could surely mean Adam, Barbara thought, every nerve tingling. But she had to make sure.

'Who is it speaking?' she asked.

'You won't know me. I work here, and he asked me to give the message.

Does it mean anything?'

Adam must have had to go out, Barbara thought, surprised. 'Yes, I suppose so,' she said doubtfully.

'He said he'll explain everything when he sees you, and you are to wait, because he may be held up. Oh, and there's one other thing I was to say — don't stop to change out of your uniform. He specially wants you to be in your uniform. Right?'

That was Adam all right, Barbara thought, in swift amusement. He had said to her once, rather severely, that the Hopwood General's uniform was some measure of protection for a young nurse, if she had to be out alone at night.

'All right, I'll go at once,' Barbara said, and rang off. Annoyed with herself for being so excited, she hastily washed, and tidied, and slipped out of the Home. She could just get a bus if she hurried.

A group of young nurses called to her. They would be wanting to see her ring, and it would make her late. It seemed safer to pretend not to hear them than to have to make awkward explanations, so Barbara hurried on.

It was cold at Church Corner, but she walked up and down, trying to keep warm, and watching every car for Adam's.

The church clock struck the half hour, three-quarters, then the hour. Still he didn't come.

Uneasily Barbara wondered what to do. The voice on the telephone hadn't said how long she was to wait, so she supposed she had better hang on for a while.

Where would he have gone, to be picking her up here? She wished she had pressed for more details, but it had seemed all right when that woman had talked to her on the telephone. Now, going over that telephone message, it had been rather vague. Where had it been coming from? Supposing something had happened to Adam? Even the Casualty Officer could get involved in a road accident, she told herself fever-ishly.

If she had had any doubts about her feelings for him before, she hadn't then. She went through a bad half hour, until she recalled that this wasn't the first time he had not appeared as arranged. It was true that he had written a message and it had miscarried, but perhaps on this occasion his verbal message had been delivered wrongly or incompletely.

So her thoughts see-sawed. Should she wait, as he had directed, or should she try to find a callbox, ring up the hospital, find out if anything had happened to him? But if nothing had, wouldn't she look rather silly, admit-ting to what was nothing more nor less than being stood up by her new fiancé?

But Adam wouldn't do that to her. And if she didn't choose to believe that he had met with an accident, then the only other alternative was that the message hadn't been from Adam at all.

But if not from Adam, then from whom?

Becoming more upset as each moment went by, Barbara at last gave up waiting, and hurried back to the hospital. She had just missed a bus, so it meant walking. She was cold and tired and very perturbed when she arrived back at the Nurses' Home, for even if it hadn't been Adam arranging that abortive wait on the Ring Road, someone had sent that message. Someone who had meant her to believe it was Adam?

The whole thing was a complete mystery, and she had no idea how to unravel it.

'Oh, there you are, Caley!' a Staff Nurse said, as she opened the main door and went into the Nurses' Home. 'You look a bit upset! What happened?'

'Happened?' she repeated, as she caught sight of her white face in a mirror.

'Yes! Mr. Thorne's been trying to contact you!'

'Mr. Thorne?' Barbara whispered. 'Where, *here?*'

'Yes, he's been on duty late, but he came over and he seemed a bit put out to find you'd gone out without telling him!'

Barbara's legs felt like jelly. So it hadn't been Adam who had sent that message! How on earth was she going to tell him what had happened? At the time it had seemed the most natural thing on earth, but now it had become completely unreal.

She must find him and get to the bottom of this. But at least he hadn't been involved in an accident. Her relief over that aspect warred with her confusion over the rest of it, and, because she was lost in thought, she almost ran full tilt into Damien Eldridge.

He caught her by the arms to steady her. 'Barbara! Where have you been?' he asked angrily. 'I've been waiting about. I felt such a fool sitting in the car outside. I drove off and kept coming back. Where have you been?'

'What are you doing here anyway?' she asked blankly. 'Did you ask someone to phone me a message?'

But of course, he hadn't. He hardly heard what she said. All he could say was that he had never waited about for anyone before in his life. He was outraged, indignant, hurt. He seemed to think that a mere nurse had no right at all to treat anyone like Damien Eldridge in such a way.

Barbara was completely at a loss to understand him. 'Damien, what's the matter with you? I can't stop now — I've got to find someone. It's urgent. Let me go!'

'No, we're having this out first,' he said, holding her firmly by the arms. 'You wouldn't stop and speak to me this afternoon, and I'm not going to be put off again! What's all this about you being engaged to someone else? You knew how I felt about you — I've made no secret of it all along, and you let me see you cared, too.'

'What are you talking about? You still belong to Margaret Knowles! And even if you didn't, I've never said — '

'Oh, no, you've never actually said! You were pretty clever there, Barbara! But you've led me on, and if anyone gives up anyone else, it's me, not the other party! No one jilts Damien Eldridge, understand?'

'You know, either I'm mad or you are!' Barbara cried. 'Everything's crazy this evening! I can't jilt you because I've never belonged to you! There's nothing between us and you know it! You bargained with me to go out with you once or twice, in return for your promise to visit Margaret! It was a disgusting arrangement, but the best I could manage. And you've no right — '

Her words were lost by a sudden exclamation from him, as he pulled her savagely to him. 'I want you!' he muttered, and he pressed her to him and his mouth came down on hers, hard. She couldn't break away. The way he held her, her arms were pinioned.

For a second she was completely taken by surprise. Then anger flooded her. First she had been duped by someone on the telephone, to stand and get cold and worried on the Ring Road, and now Damien had caught her in this dreadful position, here in the hospital grounds!

Perhaps he had thought she wouldn't struggle. He certainly loosened his hold on her, and she pushed him sharply away, but he caught her again. She struggled, and it was at that moment that Adam, making his way again to the Home to see if she had returned, came upon them.

14

'What was all that about?' Sue demanded, panting up the stairs to catch Barbara in her headlong flight. 'Wasn't that Adam Thorne and Damien out there?'

'Oh, leave me alone!' Barbara cried, pushing open her door, but Sue wasn't going to be left out of this.

'It was an awful row, wasn't it? What happened? I'd only just got back from being out with Colin all evening! What happened to you, then?'

Barbara shut the door behind Sue, to keep out the other nurses surging along the corridor, scraping into the Home at the last minute. Most of them must have heard something of what had happened outside.

'This would happen to me!' she flared. 'Oh, Sue, it's all horrible, horrible!'

'Tell me about it, then!' Sue said, exasperated.

'I'd just got back and found Damien there. He was furious about me being engaged to Adam Thorne, and he kept saying he'd made no secret of his feelings, and that he was going to get free of Margaret Knowles — oh, you don't know about any of that, do you?' she broke off, as Sue's eager smile faded. 'Honestly, Sue, I thought it was all talk. I didn't want to mention it to anyone else. I hoped I would never have to! He was engaged to Margaret Knowles, and he had no business to be thinking about breaking it up for someone else! Anyway, the long and short of it was he started kissing me and I was trying to push him away and Adam came along! He was absolutely furious!'

'Which one of them was shouting? I wonder Home Sister didn't come out!'

'It was Damien,' Barbara said. 'Adam doesn't ever shout. He just said a few short sharp words. Oh, I'll never hear the last of this!'

Sue didn't answer. Her silence was the accusing kind, which penetrated Barbara's thoughts, reminding her sharply of the fact that they had only been friends again recently, and that not so long ago this had been Sue's manner all the time, presumably because Barbara had been more friendly with Damien than the rest of them had. Damien had a lot to answer for!

'I'm sorry you didn't know about all that business, Sue,' Barbara said, biting her lip. 'I didn't mean to mention it. It slipped out. I did try to tell you at the time but, well, we weren't exactly on good terms, were we?'

Sue's frosty look didn't change. 'If you want to keep two boy-friends going, it's your look-out,' she said.

'It was no doing of mine, and I've said that to everyone, over and over again!' Barbara burst out. 'I was only trying to help. I didn't ask for any of this to happen!'

'What I can't understand is how you

came to be in a clinch with Damien, so near the Home at this time of night, when you're supposed to be engaged to Adam Thorne! I should have thought you'd have been with him all evening. Weren't you supposed to have been with him?'

'No — yes — well, no,' Barbara said incoherently, reddening. 'I went to Church Corner, on the Ring Road.'

'What on earth for?' Sue asked, staring.

'I got a message.'

'Who from?'

'I don't know! I thought it might be from Adam only — oh, it's so hard to explain!'

'What was the message, then?'

'To wait there for him, only he didn't turn up so I came back. And there was Damien waiting.' She stared at her friend. 'Don't you believe me?'

'Well, would you, if I came out with a story like that?' Sue said, turning to go. 'I don't get it, Bar. You seemed so nice at first. We've trained together for months, and I never got the slightest hint that you were like this.'

'Like what?' Barbara cried desperately. If this was how Sue was taking it — Sue, her friend and ally — how could she expect Adam to react when he heard the story?

'Like this — running several boy-friends together and getting into messes. Well, look at that rumour that was going around not long ago!'

'You never believed me, after all,' Barbara breathed.

'I did try to, Bar, but how can I? There's no smoke without fire. That's what everyone says.'

It was almost time for lights out. Sue hurried away and Barbara hastily undressed.

Her head was aching. She remembered she had had no food. It had been a most unpleasant, unnerving evening.

She lay for a long time staring at the ceiling. Adam had coldly dispatched her into the Home, saying he would talk to her in the morning.

There had been no chance at all to explain to him then, and perhaps it was as well. That story must be told more smoothly to Adam tomorrow, unless she wanted to risk his being as unbelieving as Sue had been.

And yet, what was the truth? Clearly Adam hadn't sent that message. He had been looking for her. It appeared that he hadn't been out at all!

Equally clearly, Damien hadn't caused it to be sent. Then who had?

She went to sleep promising herself that she would go over early and try to get a word with Adam. She must get to the bottom of this, in case such a thing happened again.

But in the morning Barbara got no chance to speak to Adam, for yet another rumour broke. The flat of Russell Mallory, the screen star that Barbara had met at that noisy party given for Damien on his return from convalescence, had been burgled, and the thief — a girl — had been disturbed by the porter, but she had got away by hurling a cushion in his face and putting the lights out. The porter, however, had got a good look at her. She had been young, fair, very pretty and . . . wearing the uniform of a nurse at the Hopwood General Hospital.

★ ★ ★

Barbara thought that as long as she lived, she would never get over that dreadful day, with its highlight the building up of the rumour. The same suspicious, covert glances in her direction. The snatches of conversation she heard as she went about her work.

'They say this girl didn't take anything of value,' Barbara heard someone say, on the other side of a partition. 'The porter disturbed her before she could, I suppose!'

'Where did you hear that, then?'

'Oh, from the porter when he was in here this morning — he burnt his hand, stoking the boiler in the basement. No one would have heard a thing about it, if he hadn't told everyone, because the owner of the flat tried to keep it all quiet.'

'Why? Why didn't he call the police?'

'Search me! He was hot on keeping the police out, the porter said. (I heard him!) I expect that film star had something to hide, anyway. They're all alike, my father says. Still, that porter did keep saying that if he saw this nurse, he'd know her. He got a good look at her.'

Barbara felt sick. It seemed that everyone was talking about it, as if they enjoyed the subject.

Later, when she was scrubbing mackintoshes, she heard two juniors talking. 'Well,' said one, 'it isn't the first time something like this has happened, is it?'

'No-o,' the other one said doubtfully, 'but if she was going to break into someone's flat, what did the chump want to go in uniform for?'

'No one said she *broke in*. That's just it! She had a key!' the other junior squealed. 'As to her uniform, every-one's saying she probably used it as a cover. When she left here, it would look as if she was just going out for a quiet walk, and the same when she came back. All innocent, see? My mother says it's always the quiet ones you can't trust! Who'd have thought it of *her?* She always seemed so nice.'

'But we don't know it *was* her, do we?' the other girl objected. 'Just because she was not very tall, and fair and pretty, well, that might be any one of dozens!'

'Except that it was just one of that description that there was a rumour about before,' the other girl reminded her. 'And they're also saying that what she was really after was a bundle of letters.'

'Letters! But who would care about letters?'

'Don't be a simpleton! When people steal letters it usually means they're being *blackmailed*!'

'Oh, now look — that sort of thing

happens *on* the films, not in private life. Besides, which young nurse here would have that sort of thing going on in her free hours?'

'She's had everything else!' the other retorted. 'Film star friends, wild parties, trips out in that car of his and now she's engaged to you-know-who, who's filthy rich!'

'Shut up — someone will hear you!' the other girl said.

Barbara felt sick. The message she had received now had a new significance. Clearly it had not had its origin with either Damien or Adam. But who — *who* could have been responsible for it? Who, in all this hospital, could possibly have wanted her to be on that cold corner of the Ring Road, *in uniform,* she remembered, last night? What was the purpose of it? If someone in this hospital had wanted to take some letters from someone's flat, why involve Barbara at all?

This time the rumour didn't end there. There was, of course, the interview with Matron, who gave nothing away. If she disbelieved Barbara's story, she didn't say so; but she wasn't satisfied, that much was obvious. Adam Thorne, too, gave very little away, but to Barbara it was obvious that he didn't believe her story.

'I've told you all I know!' she said desperately. 'I know nothing whatever about Russell Mallory's flat! I wouldn't even know where it was!'

'But you did know Russell Mallory, I believe?'

'I met him at that horrid party,' she agreed.

'And you didn't know his flat was in the same block?' Adam asked mildly.

'No! I've told you I didn't! If only I could think who sent that message to me!' she cried, her head in her hands.

'What I don't understand,' Adam said, marching up and down the sitting-room of the Nurses' Home where he had arranged to talk to her, 'is why you should ever think I would be discourteous enough to ask someone else to telephone you, or indeed to expect you to wait, alone — at night — in that unpleasant spot?'

Barbara felt he had flicked her with a whip, and her nerves were already at snapping point.

'Oh, wouldn't you?' she flared. 'I don't know! You do some extremely unpredictable things, I would have said! Such as for instance ordering me to force a person to come and visit a patient, to the extent of my having to go to those horrible parties. And also such as telling a patient quite unexpectedly that you were engaged to be married to me! I think I would expect anything of someone who did things like that and thought nothing of it!'

His silence and the way he stared at her, reduced her to a very small size. 'I'm sorry,' she said. 'That was rude, and I didn't mean to be. At the same time, I think it's unfair that all this should happen to me. I've done nothing to deserve it. And I have no — no alibi, I believe it's called — no one knows I was freezing on the Ring Road when all this was supposed to be happening.'

'It's going to be tricky,' he said at last. 'Seeing's believing, so they say. A lot of people saw you go out in a hurry, Bar, in your uniform. I suppose a fair number saw you with Eldridge. What I saw didn't please me, though you've explained it away. But what the eye sees is the lasting image, you know.'

'That means you don't believe me,' she said dully. And when he didn't answer to that, she said, 'You can believe I would be idiotic enough to write damaging letters in the first place to a man like Russell Mallory — '

'But you said you didn't know the man!' he swiftly took her up.

'That's true. I just met him at that party. He tried to flirt with me on the strength of five minutes' acquaintance — it was enough for me to form an opinion,' she said crisply. 'And there's another thing: if you really believed I would write those letters, you surely don't think I'd be mad enough to go openly to his flat — in uniform — to try to steal them back! And where would I have found the time for this hectic existence I'm supposed to have lived, during which those letters were written?'

He turned away from her. He was hating every minute of this. 'Don't talk such nonsense, Barbara. I'm trying to help you. I had hoped you'd have something quite different to say, by way of accounting for your movements last night, but how can I go to Matron and tell her that I think it quite feasible that you should receive an odd message like that, and moreover, that you would promptly go and wait (without telling a soul about it!) in such an improbable spot! You must have known it wouldn't be from me, a message like that!'

'I know it sounds mad now, but at the time it seemed likely. No more unlikely, anyway, than you — who were supposed to be engaged to me! — clearing off as you did, without even saying good night to me!' she couldn't resist adding.

He came and leaned over her. 'Bar, the Super came and fetched me, to discuss a one-time patient. It happens sometimes, and I somehow don't feel that the Super would like it if his Casualty Officer asked permission to kiss his fiancée good night first.'

'Now you're making fun of me!' she said furiously. 'Anyway, now's as good a time as any for you to put an end to this silly farce, isn't it?'

'On the contrary,' he said coolly, straightening up. 'The way I see it, it gives me a good excuse for carrying on with our engagement. Loyalty to my fiancée, for a start!'

She flushed miserably. So he was going to be punctilious in this piece of acting, because of the new rumour! What a hateful business it all was!

'Well, as you won't budge from that story of yours about the telephone message,' he sighed at last, 'we can only wait for Matron to act. She's going to publicly invite the guilty nurse to come secretly to her office and confess. No one will know which one it was.'

Matron called the nurses together and talked very seriously to them, calling their attention to the good name of the hospital in the past, and begging the guilty party to own up. But no one took advantage of her promise. And so the rumours reverted to Barbara, and she knew that everyone was sure she was at the bottom of it, just as they believed she had been last time, and that the Casualty Officer had vouched for her because he knew he was going to ask her to marry him.

But because the Casualty Dept. was so short-staffed, Barbara was allowed to go on working, but the Superintendent was pressing Matron to do something about it. The nursing staff was her responsibility, and just because this girl happened to be engaged to the Casualty Officer (who also happened to be one of the Thorne family and of local importance) didn't mean, he averred, that the good name of the hospital could be dragged in the mud.

So it was arranged that the porter of the block of flats, when he came to have his hand dressed the next morning, should have the opportunity of seeing Barbara, without being forewarned. If he recognised her, then she would have to go, but if he didn't, it would at least clear her name, and they would have to look elsewhere for the culprit.

Neither Adam Thorne nor Barbara knew of this. Only Matron and the Superintendent, and Sister Casualty, who in her heart was very glad that something active was being done. She liked Barbara and it grieved her to think that of all people on the nursing staff, little Nurse Caley appeared to be the only one in any way harmed by the invasion of the film world in the person of Damien Eldridge.

Barbara's duties the next morning were stocking and sterilising, but Sister Casualty sent her with a message to Adam, who was dressing the burnt hand of the porter of the block of flats. She herself was helping the Staff nurse with a young baby in a cubicle near enough to see what was going on.

The porter was still full of the story of the girl he had seen. 'It's the rummiest thing!' he confided to Adam. 'Me being here with this burnt hand, I mean! It was the last thing I expected, to be in the very hospital where that girl was working! I'll never get over it if I live to be a hundred. Fancy doing the job in full uniform, that's what I can't understand! I mean, it's such a — well, I mean, you can't miss that uniform!'

'Distinctive,' Adam suggested, thinking all the time of Barbara, and that mysterious telephone call.

'That's it!' the porter agreed. 'But just let me set eyes on that young woman, that's all! I'd know her anywhere! That colour hair — '

That was when Barbara came in. She came completely disinterested, so far as the patient was concerned. It was Adam who claimed all her attention. Adam, whose smile could make her pulse leap and race; whose frown brought the lump into her throat, and reminded her that he wasn't really hers, and that this engagement of theirs would be broken, perhaps sooner than she knew.

The porter half rose in his chair. 'But that's her! That's the one!' he gasped. 'Well, knock me down with a feather, it's her all right! You near knocked me flat with that cushion last night, my beauty!' he roared at Barbara.

She looked blankly at him until he mentioned the cushion, but realisation of his identity dawned on her then.

She looked at Adam in alarm. 'Is this the porter?'

He nodded. She saw he looked distressed. He would have given the world to have avoided this. He had thought she was safely in the stock-room this morning, during the porter's visit.

'I've never seen him in my life before!' she gasped.

Adam rose to his feet, anger in his

310

face, as he saw Sister Casualty looking. In that moment he guessed that this had been arranged, but he could do nothing.

'Don't come that with me!' the porter said, equally angry, but in his case it was because his word was being doubted. 'I can prove it. I noticed something else about you — something you'll have hard work to explain away! Hah, didn't think I was that observant, did you, near knocking me out with a cushion, but I noticed. Here, stand over there — now I'd be on the floor like this, where I staggered — '

'Be careful of that hand of yours!' Adam warned.

'Never mind my hand, guv, we've got to get this settled. Now, let's see your right leg, Nurse.'

Barbara looked indignant, but stood where she was. The porter's jaw dropped. 'But there was a mark there last night — a sort of big brown mole. Beauty spot, don't you call it? I noticed it particularly!'

'Well, as you will see, this nurse hasn't a blemish on either of her legs,' Adam said icily.

'She could cover it up, couldn't she?' the porter objected.

Sister Casualty joined them. 'We'd better clear this up on the instant, Nurse. I'm sure you've no objection to allowing this man to see how wrong he is about the presence of a mole on your leg? Now, where would you say it was?' she demanded.

The porter gulped. 'There, just above the right ankle, Sister. Well, if it isn't this nurse, then it was her double, that's all I can say! But I noticed that brown mole in particular and I thought to myself then, ah, I've got you! You can't disguise that!'

Sister Casualty looked in near triumph at Adam. She had been praying that the porter would fail in his identification, and he had!

But so far as Barbara was concerned, it didn't ease the situation, for, with a rush, several things occurred to her,

312

things she should have remembered before, and she also knew who it was that the porter had seen in Russell Mallory's flat.

'I don't think it was a nurse at all,' she told Adam, after they were free of their interviews with Matron and the superintendent. 'I think it was someone in the film company. I suppose she did it for a joke, but Matron has forbidden me to take it further. It's enough for her that there isn't a double of me on the nursing staff here.'

'I know. She told me. I wish you'd forget it now, Bar,' he said earnestly. 'Promise me you won't go rushing off if any other messages are supposed to come from me?'

'But supposing you have to send me a message?' she protested.

'I'll send it by someone we both know, if I can't speak to you on the telephone myself,' he told her. 'Now — let's forget this whole nasty business, shall we? You're cleared of this rumour, and I'll see that nothing else happens like it!'

But he hadn't seemed to realise, she thought ruefully, that without knowing why the rumour had started at first, no one could prevent a recurrence. And Barbara felt in her heart that there would be no peace for her, nor a complete clearance of the doubts in the minds of other people, if she didn't discover that reason. She had an enemy, that was clear . . .

Damien was the person to ask, she felt. He would be there that afternoon to see Margaret. Barbara promised herself she'd arrange with someone to tell her when he came out, so that she could have a word with him at the main door.

Damien came earlier today. He was still smarting over Barbara and her engagement to the Casualty Officer. He had nothing personally against Adam Thorne. It was Barbara he hated now, for what he termed cheating. She had cheated him, played an underhand game. Anyone else might have felt a flick of amusement, for Fate's paying back in the same coin — he had taken Adam's girl-friend in the past, and now Adam had robbed him of Barbara. But not Damien: there was no real humour in Damien. Other people could be hurt, but he, Damien Eldridge, mustn't be hurt. Everything had to go as he wanted it. He would never forgive Barbara for that.

Today, Margaret seemed almost desirable to him. The bandages were off her head, and her pretty honey-gold hair — so like Barbara's — was attractively arranged. Her face, now almost healed, had lost a lot of the angry colour, and was hardly notice-able until he came close to her. With plastic surgery, he realised with swift relief, she might almost be again as attractive as she once was. And she had a lot of money . . .

He set out to be really nice to her. 'That's a poppet of a garment you're flaunting, sweetheart,' he told her, and bent to kiss her.

She moved her face away slightly. 'Don't!' she said sharply.

'Don't you want me to kiss you, darling?'

'Not today, Damien. Not until I give you some news. Then I don't think you'll want to kiss me.'

'What d'you mean, Margaret? We're still engaged, you know!'

'No, Damien. Not any more,' she said, and pulled off the ring he had given her. 'Funny, I never did care for that ring. Oh, well, now you can have it back.'

'Margaret, you must be joking!' he said, laughing a little. 'This is your old Damien, remember? The one you've been — '

'Making such a fuss about?' she finished for him, as he broke off in sharp confusion. 'The one I've been crying about? No, darling, even I couldn't be such a fool as that!'

'Margaret, I swear there's nothing in what they say about that nurse — Barbara Caley! I swear it! She was film struck, wanted a screen test! I told her about us — she knew about us — '

'It's not about Barbara Caley,' Margaret told him, an aggravating smile on her lips. 'It's nothing to do with her. The situation's changed in the last few days, Damien, and I've seen someone else. I've realised what I've missed in not meeting him before, but I'm not going to let the chance go by.'

'Someone else?' he stuttered. 'Oh, rubbish! I don't believe it! How could you?'

'That's not very nice of you to remind me of what my face looks like, but as it happens, it doesn't bother him. You see, he's the person who's going to put it right again. My plastic surgeon. You see?'

It took some time to convince Damien, but she did it in the end, and he left her at last, in a towering fury. It was unfortunate for Barbara that she chose that moment to ask him for the information she so badly needed.

He stared unbelieving at her. To think

that Barbara, who had treated him like that, could believe that he would help her!

'Sorry, sweetie,' he said, carelessly, 'but I can't help you! I must rush now. 'Bye!'

She couldn't believe it. He knew the answer she wanted; he could have helped her to clear up finally what was behind this puzzling, unpleasant business, she told herself, but he wouldn't.

She watched him go into a telephone booth. He looked really savage as he dialled the number, and there was a bitter smile on his face as he talked. She turned away, deeply disappointed, but if she had known whom he was calling, her emotions would have been deeper than disappointment.

'Honey,' Damien said to the person at the other end, 'you are in trouble. It appears that the little nurse and the porter were more observant than you expected. Yes, J know, but listen. I'll help you. Will you listen, honey!'

With difficulty, he persuaded the

voice to be quiet, while he talked. 'I know we're not very good friends, but I mean to help you over this. Never mind why — I have my reasons. But meantime, for pity's sake, cover up that mole on your leg. I don't care what with — pink plaster, make-up, anything, but hide it from view! That's all!'

'But all my friends know about it!'

'Then,' he said, drawing a deep breath, 'if anything is said by someone who knows about it, I'll give you an alibi. I'll say you were with me at the time.'

15

Although she was by no means happy about the way it had all ended, yet Barbara was relieved to find that her name was cleared. The whole hospital knew now that she wasn't to blame. People kept stopping her to say they were glad, and Sue was friends with her again.

'Well, you certainly live!' Sue exclaimed, after Barbara had told her about that distressing scene with the porter of the block of flats, down in Casualty. 'Who do you think it really was impersonating you?'

'Oh, it doesn't matter any longer, does it? The whole point is, if it was someone in the film company, it wouldn't be difficult to get hold of a uniform that looked enough like ours to convince people. After all, if you see a nurse, you don't think that it's someone impersonating a nurse with a 'prop' costume, do you? You think what you're meant to, that you're seeing a real nurse! I suppose it's natural!'

'Um, yes, I see what you mean!' Sue agreed. 'Well, for goodness sake, don't go haring off again if you get one of those stupid messages!'

The animosity seemed to have gone out of everyone. Margaret, glowingly happy over her swift new friendship with her plastic surgeon, was as nice to Adam as when she had first met him. Adam found himself telling her about the scandal.

'That sounds like my friends in Damien's company!' she commented grimly. 'That certainly sounds like them! They play very rough, you know, when they feel someone is treading on their toes. I've got used to them. I play rough myself. I played rough with Damien, but he can take it! If I were you, though, I'd look out for that little Barbara of yours. She's sugar and spice — no match for Damien and his pals!'

'I wish you'd suggest what I might do, Margaret, to protect Barbara,' Adam said, in a heartfelt voice. 'I won't pretend I'm not worried about her. She's so willing, she doesn't stop to think before she acts.'

'I quite like her,' Margaret said, thinking. 'I'll do a bit of telephoning, if you like, and see if I can stop the nonsense, because you and I know very well it isn't over yet! Leave it to me, Adam!'

When Adam left her, she was calling up Buck Tragman. Buck had no terrors for Margaret. She had never danced to his tune, even though she had wanted a part in the film. She had too much money to care.

The porter from the block of flats had come back again. His hand was giving him trouble. He sat waiting patiently to see Adam, and while he waited, he sat reading about the film stars who were friends of Russell Mallory. It was an old film magazine, much dog-eared, but it passed the time.

There was a picture of Russell, looking very much the man-about-town, with the roving eye and rather cruel mouth. There was, too, a group of people behind the scenes; the director and his wife, the producer, the continuity girl, a cameraman. Taken on location, during the making of the company's last film. The background was a native village in Africa. Buck Tragman and the other males were hot and dirty and didn't appear to care. Buck Tragman's wife Romany looked less glamorous than usual, too. Her dress wasn't quite as immaculate as it was when she was in England; she wore very little make-up, native sandals and bare legs.

The porter leapt up, his eyes starting. 'It's her!' he gasped. 'Lumme, guv, I want my head searching! I've seen her a hundred times — must have! — but I never thought! Look, this one here — doesn't she look like that little nurse?' he demanded of Adam, who had just come down from seeing Margaret. 'Look, and there's the mole on her leg, I told you about! I knew I wasn't seeing things! So that's who it was! Cor, what d'you make of that?'

Sister Casualty, the Staff nurse, and several other patients crowded round him. It was unbelievable but if he could clear up the business to everyone's satisfaction, that was all they asked.

'Here, let me see that magazine,' Adam demanded, taking it from him. 'What have you come back for, anyway? Hand troubling you? Well, perhaps Sister would look at it, till I come back. There's something I must do!'

He strode back the way he had come, to Margaret's room, coat tails flying, a very grim look on his face.

Margaret was lying very still, the telephone to her ear; not talking, just listening to a medley of shouting voices at the other end. When she saw Adam, she put her finger to her lips to caution him to be quiet. Then she beckoned to him to bend over while she put the phone to his ear for a second or so. Then she took it back, and went on listening.

He pulled a face, and raised his eyebrows, but there was a sharp crack, and then the dialling tone. Regretfully Margaret replaced the receiver.

'I think he must have thrown the telephone at her,' she said. 'Oh, I did enjoy that! It's a long time since I've listened in to such a good row.'

'Who on earth was it?'

'Buck Tragman, the director of Damien's film company. And his wife, Romany.' Her lips curled in a smile of sheer amusement. 'He's very jealous of her. Gets quite violent if he thinks she's been unfaithful. She usually manages to hide her larks. However, I called him up and suggested that Romany was having a *strong friendship* with Russell Mallory. That was all I needed to say. Romany must have been in the room with him because he left off talking to me and turned to her. He shouted at her and she screamed back at him. Such fun! He forgot I was still on the other end of the line.'

'But how did you know, Margaret?' Adam asked, and passed the magazine over to her, opened at the page with the picture. 'The porter's just found it — he says that's the woman who was dressed as a nurse!'

'The mole on her leg! I'd forgotten that!' Margaret said surprised. 'Oh, well, that rather clinches it, doesn't it? I was only guessing. You see, if she's been silly enough to write letters to Russell Mallory (and she's quite likely to, being love-starved) he's such a wretch, he wouldn't hesitate to hold them over her. She wouldn't like that. She'd be driven to try and get them back. She *is* very much like your Barbara, you know, enough to get the idea of dressing up as a nurse. Oh, yes, it all fits, don't you think?'

'Well, if you say so, but I confess I'm quite out of my depth with people who will do such things!' Adam snorted. 'It seems a most remarkable way of going on!'

'You're so conventional, darling,'

Margaret smiled. 'I could tell you of things that have happened, that would completely stagger you! But you haven't heard everything about this yet, have you? You see, Romany told her husband she was with Damien at the time! Damien came to see me yesterday and I told him I was in love with my plastic surgeon, so that makes two things to make poor Damien very angry. How he will hate everyone! He likes things to go as he plans them.'

'What's the significance of all that, Margaret?'

'Well, d'you see, he won't have time to properly enjoy hating me for yesterday, before he gets into trouble with Buck Tragman. And I don't think it was true — I really believe Romany was in Russell Mallory's flat throwing cushions at the porter, and not with Damien at all. I wonder which of those two silly men Buck Tragman will go for? He's rather a bully and a brute when he gets really upset over Romany.'

Adam found the whole thing very

distasteful. He was determined to warn Barbara about not seeing those film people any more, at the earliest moment.

He pulled up sharply, and stood staring out of the corridor window. There were several things he had forgotten. He couldn't very well warn Barbara with any hope of her taking any notice of him; it was a sham engagement between them, giving him no rights of any kind, and now that Margaret was interested in her surgeon and didn't care what happened to Damien Eldridge, Barbara would be the first to point out that their engagement could be terminated. There was now no further need for it, from Barbara's point of view.

He felt sick at the thought. So much had happened in the last forty-eight hours that he hadn't really examined this new aspect at all, and he had certainly had no opportunity of telling Barbara that Margaret had fallen in love with her new surgeon!

For the hundredth time, Adam asked himself just what Barbara's feelings for Damien Eldridge really were. Had she meant it when she had told him that Damien had seemed rather artificial against his own background, at that disastrous party she had been enveigled into attending? Or had she just said it, because she knew that he didn't like Damien and would be angry to think Barbara was taking Margaret's man away from her?

He couldn't find the answer to all that. He only knew he loved Barbara so much that his own feelings frightened him.

He went back to Casualty, still undecided as to what course to take. He ought, of course, to tell Barbara about Margaret not wanting Damien any more, and give Barbara the chance of making up her own mind. But it wasn't going to be easy. Barbara would want to know when he had first discovered Margaret's true feelings. That had been on the same day that he had announced his engagement to Barbara. Barbara would want to know why he hadn't told her at once.

It had been no surprise to him, to find that Margaret was interested in her new surgeon, or he in her. Adam had seen that first flare of interest leap into Margaret's eyes when he had taken the great man in and introduced the patient. At the time he had been so relieved to find that Margaret had decided to drop her mood of opposition to every new treatment suggested, that he had accepted it with delight.

But it wouldn't be easy to make Barbara see all that from his point of view. She didn't know he loved her, and in his heart he considered he would have a great difficulty in convincing her of that. And if, as he suspected, she still secretly loved Damien Eldridge, then she wouldn't care. She would just demand the termination of Adam's engagement to her.

There was a big explosion in one of the new factories that afternoon. He had no chance to speak to Barbara, and he was still rushing about when she went off duty. He had no idea what she was going to do or where he could find her.

When he did get free, he found she had gone out and no one seemed to know where. In desperation he searched for Sue Gardner, remembering that Sue and Barbara were friends again. Sue was walking along laughing and talking with another nurse. When he called to her, the other girl tactfully left her. Sue stood stock-still, staring at him as if he were a ghost.

'You still here, Mr. Thorne?' she asked blankly.

'What d'you mean, *still here?*' he demanded.

'But you said on the telephone — '

His heart lurched. 'Say that again!' he thundered.

'Didn't you telephone to Barbara?'

'No, I didn't! I haven't been out of Casualty for hours! Where *is* Barbara?'

'She went — where you said she was

to go! At least, I thought it was you — '

'My God!' he groaned. 'I told her and told her she wasn't to take any notice of requests by telephone to go anywhere!'

'But she didn't. She didn't even go to the telephone. I gave her the message,' Sue said, looking really scared.

'Now look — tell me about it from the beginning. Don't miss anything out, but don't be too long. I've got to find Barbara!'

Sue drew a deep breath. 'Well, someone came and said the Casualty Officer was on the phone for Barbara. She wasn't there so I went to answer it for her. And I thought it was you, too — it sounded as like as you are now!'

'Go on!'

'Well, you — I mean he, whoever it was, said 'Where's Barbara?' Honestly, it sounded just like you when — well, when you're being a bit sharp! Sorry, but you did say — '

'All right! Go on! What happened then?'

'I said she wasn't there and could I take a message. He said, 'All right, tell her to go down to the gates. One of the cars will pick her up, from the film company. I'm there now, at the studios. We'll get to the bottom of this!' '

'But you said you thought it was me!' Adam stormed.

'That's right! It sounded like you. I thought you meant you were on to something new about what had happened. Anyway, I knew you'd said she wasn't to go anywhere so I reminded him. And this is what made me think it must be you.'

'Go on!'

'Well, he said, 'Who is it speaking? It sounds like Nurse Gardner!' Well, when he knew my name, can you blame me for being convinced it was you? Then he said, 'Look, I know all about that, but it is me on the telephone. Tell Barbara so, and tell her to look sharp!' '

'My heavens!' He stared at Sue. 'Someone who knows us all well enough to be convincing. I'll get my car. Come with me, will you?'

'But where are you going?'

'To the film studios, of course!'

'But Mr. Thorne — ' Sue began, running to keep up with him.

'Well, what is it, Nurse?'

'I was thinking — we don't know that she's gone to the film studios, do we?'

'But you said just now — '

'I know I said, but look at it this way! It wasn't you on the telephone — it was someone else — he just wanted Barbara to get into that car he was sending, with a stranger at the wheel, thinking it was from the studios. Well, I don't want to be a wet blanket, but honestly, she could have been driven wherever he wanted her to go, after she'd once got in that car, couldn't she?'

'I see what you mean!'

'Should we call the police?' Sue asked in a small voice. He took her by the shoulders. 'Think, Nurse, think! You were the only one to hear that voice — '

'No. The maid heard it too — '

'Well, she wouldn't know. But you

might — think! Who could it have been, who could make his voice sound like mine, who would know sufficient about the hospital to know it was you taking the call for Barbara, and who'd know about the hospital gates? Who *might* it have been, now you know for sure that it wasn't me?'

Sue thought, wrinkling her brows. Then she said, 'Well, it might have been Damien Eldridge. I don't know — you're putting the thought into my head. But it *might* have been . . . '

'He's an actor. He knows a lot about us. He just could be at the back of that other telephone call last week!' He sounded terribly angry. 'Let's go back to the hospital and call up the studios. They might know where he'd be.'

It took a little time to find the number but when they did get through to the studios it was to learn that there had been high words between Damien and his director about Romany Tragman; high words which had ended with Buck Tragman beating Damien up.

Damien had gone off somewhere in his car. The Tragmans had also left the studio.

'What on earth is going on?' Adam muttered, as he replaced the receiver, and told Sue what he had heard.

'There really isn't anything for it but to telephone the police!'

'What will you tell them?' Sue murmured. 'That we think she's gone off with a film star she's been out with before?'

'That she's been hoaxed into believing she was being taken to meet me!' he retorted. 'I know we don't know she'll come to any harm, but anyone who would play that sort of game can't mean to do her any good, I should think!'

Sister Casualty came over then. She was looking for him. 'Oh, Mr. Thorne, I'm so glad I found you!' she said. 'Can you come and meet an ambulance coming in? I know you're not on call, but I think you might want to be in on this.'

Sue was aware that her heart was beating with a sickening irregular thudding. She stole a look at Adam Thorne and noticed the way his face changed. They were both thinking the same thing.

'What is it, then, Sister?' he asked, in a strained voice unlike his own. 'If it isn't urgent — that fact is, we're trying to find Nurse Caley!'

'This is ... Nurse Caley,' she faltered.

★   ★   ★

The car drew up to the kerb as Barbara shot out of the main gates of the hospital. There was a man in chauffeur's uniform at the wheel. It was, in fact, a car she recognised as belonging to the studios.

She had no reason to be in doubt. Sue had told her that she had actually spoken to Adam Thorne on the telephone. It was like Adam to take himself off to the film studios and get everything straightened out. He was, she knew, rankling just as much as she was, over this puzzling business. She would be thankful to find out the truth.

And so she got into the car without an uneasy thought. The man leaned over and opened the back door for her, and if he had omitted a courtesy in not getting out and coming round to hold it open and close it, she put it down to the jam of traffic outside the hospital and his anxiety to get away without delay.

He drove quickly and smoothly, threading the difficult streets of Hopwood with care. Not until they reached the sharp turn at the last traffic lights did she have any doubt that they were going to the studios.

'You should have turned right here, shouldn't you?' she leaned over to ask the man.

No one ever really looks at a hired driver's face. Until then, she had been conscious of a dark jacket, a peaked cap, and because the man had been sitting at the wheel and she had been instructed to expect a chauffeur-driven car, she had taken it for granted that this was, indeed, just a chauffeur.

Now that she came to look closely at that profile, she realised uneasily that she had made a mistake. She looked into the driving mirror, and met the eyes of Damien Eldridge.

'Damien!' she whispered. 'What's the idea? What are you playing at, dressed up as a chauffeur?'

He went on grimly driving. Then she noticed the bruises on his cheek-bones, and saw the cut down one side of his eye.

'What happened to your face?' she gasped.

'Buck Tragman got annoyed with me,' he said, between his teeth. 'He does get annoyed with people sometimes. He is a rough, uncouth man. I hate him.'

'Yes, but why? Oh, stop the car, Damien, and explain — I don't understand any of this! Where are we going? Sue said Mr. Thorne wanted me to go to the studios.'

'Aren't we being rather formal? *Mr.* Thorne? Come now — surely you call your fiancé by his Christian name?'

'Damien, stop the car! Turn round or something! He'll be wondering where I am!'

'Really, Nurse, you forget yourself!' Damien said, in perfect mimicry of Adam's rather deep, formal voice.

Her eyes met his in the driving mirror. 'You! It was you on the telephone!'

'I am an actor,' he told her simply, with as much dignity and pride as if he had announced himself to be an emperor.

'But why, why? Why did you send that message on the telephone? Where is Adam?'

'I've no idea, sweetie. I only know that I'm fed up with everyone! No one's going to give Damien Eldridge the run-around, and they needn't think it. So you and I are going to a nice little place I know, to have a nice quiet talk, a little intimate dinner, and ... the pleasure you've promised me, time and again, and never kept your word.'

'You must be mad! I've never promised you anything!'

'Oh, yes, you have — with your eyes, if not with actual words. You don't have to put things in writing for me to catch on, sweetie.'

'Are you going to turn round and go back?' she stormed.

'You heard what I said!' His mouth was smiling, but there was a steely quality in his voice that assured her he wasn't playing. Whether he believed he could persuade her to do as he had suggested, or whether he thought he could achieve his object by force, she had no idea. Of one thing she could be sure, and that was, he wasn't going to turn back now, just because she asked him to.

'You're rather a silly sweetie, you know,' he went on. 'All you had to do was to be nice to me, and then I'd have let you go. I never hang on to a girl, once she's been sweet to me. But to refuse me, and go and get engaged to someone else without even telling me — well, that wasn't nice!'

'I think you're mad!' she said again, but she knew, even as she said it, that this was his usual procedure and she ought to have known it. He had become engaged to Margaret because she had money and at the time he had badly needed it. He hadn't expected her to want to hang on to him, and he had wriggled like a worm on the hook. Hadn't he made a play for Barbara, even while Margaret was desperately ill in hospital? That ought to have warned her that he had no conscience or any ethics to speak of. He did as he pleased, and believed it to be right.

'Stop the car, Damien! I'll get out and find some way of getting back to Hopwood!' she said furiously.

'Darling, you are getting rather boring,' he said. But she saw now that he wasn't going to be moved from his fixed intention.

'All right,' she said. 'Where is the place you are taking me?' If she could just know their route, she might find a set of traffic lights where they would have to slow down, and she could jump out.

'Let it be a nice surprise,' Damien said aggravatingly.

As he said it, he swung off the highway down a secondary road. Trees and hedges, a deep ditch, and not a soul in sight, she saw, with growing despondency. And they were travelling far too fast for her to open a door and jump out.

Now she would have to take her chance. Sooner or later he would have to slow down at a major road sign and that would be the opportunity she needed!

She quietly tried to open the door beside her, but she couldn't make the catch work. Damien realised what she was doing. 'Cut it out!' he barked, and did something to the catch on his own door. 'That's locked all the doors, so you'd better sit still till we arrive.'

Barbara sat back, shaking all over. There must be something she could do! Beneath that quiet exterior, the temper and spirited disposition that Adam had discovered, boiled up. Flinging caution to the winds, she jumped up, leaned over the seat, and grabbed the steering-wheel.

It caught Damien by surprise, but he was a good driver. He threw out an arm, pushing her back, and at the same time swung the wheel over. Given ordinary luck, he might have regained the steering, but three things were against him. They were coming to a junction of the type Barbara had been praying for, a junction which led to a main road one way and a railway bridge the other. Coming over the bridge was a farm wagon, and blinding him by the head-lamps was a heavy-loaded lorry from the main road.

Desperate, he swung left, and the door which Barbara had been wrestling with, and which had half opened, now flew wide, and she was thrown out.

With a scream, she found she was catapulted down the bank where the wire mesh fence stopped her, knocking the breath out of her body.

She lay there, in a crouching position, one leg buckled under her. Something sharp was pressing on her forehead, and wet trickled down her face. She put up a shaking hand to touch it. It came away wet and red.

The crashing and grinding and splintering noises suddenly stopped, and there was a sharp silence. She forced herself to look upwards. Damien's car had run up the bank, the bonnet crushed into the brickwork at the end of the bridge. Running figures came from the lorry and the farm cart, towards the car, and the inert figure of Damien, thrown like a rag doll to hang half out of the crazily open door. No one seemed to know about Barbara, she thought, as the darkness closed down on her and she lost consciousness.

There had been many times in her short period in the Casualty Department of the Hopwood General Hospital that Barbara had wondered what the patient felt, being brought in from a road accident.

Her own impressions were limited. She remembered being lifted out of the ambulance and Casualty Sister standing there, large and plump and comfortable, looking, Barbara thought in stupefaction, as if she were going to burst into tears at any minute. What an absurd thought, she told herself! Someone who looked very much like Sue, ran forward, frankly crying, and saying: 'Bar!' just as Sue often did. But Sue wouldn't be down here in Casualty. That was absurd thought No. 2. Most absurd of all was someone she took to be Adam Thorne, his face creased in anguish as he came forward to help with the stretcher.

How, she asked herself, could Adam

be here? He hadn't got a white coat on. He was in a rough woolly sweater which she hadn't seen before, with a polo collar, and his hair looked dishevelled. Never had she seen his hair looking anything but slick and tidy.

Her next impression was of the theatre, seen from the operating table. The patient's-eye-view. The big central light blinded her, and the glitter of the instruments laid out in neat order caught the light and winked back at her. Little transient views that convinced her that she was truly dreaming.

The patches in between were thick and dense, like being in a fog. Snatches of voices, split-second impressions of hands doing things, putting a dressing on her head, adjusting the pulley to her leg — or was it both legs? And pain — terrifying pain — tore at her, chasing her to the welcome oblivion and darkness again.

She came to one day to find herself crying a name. 'Damien, Damien!' and finding Adam sitting beside her.

'Hush, my darling, it's all right,' she thought she heard him say.

That was the thing she had dreamed of him saying, only it was just a pretend engagement. 'Damien, Damien,' she said again.

No one understood that she wasn't wanting Damien there. No one seemed to realise that she just wanted to know what had happened to him. Her mouth felt stiff and strange and her tongue wouldn't work. Fear chased all over her and held her in its grip. What had happened to her?

She looked at the apparatus above her bed. She was in a small room. She felt as trussed as a chicken. A curious thud-thudding noise grew steadily louder, until she realised that it was merely her own heart.

'Is Damien dead?' she managed at last. Three words forced out of her because it was imperative that she had to know.

'No, he's doing fine,' someone said, only it wasn't Adam this time but the

R.S.O. The Sister who had been so glad to see her that first day she had visited Margaret Knowles, stood anxiously behind him, and put in quickly, 'He'll be along to see you when he's well enough. You are not to worry about anything.'

'Don't want to see him,' Barbara said, but they were moving away and hadn't appeared to hear.

She knew she was desperately ill because she was never left alone. It was usually a little junior sitting by her, anxiously doing her first 'special-ing' job. Sometimes it was Adam, but Barbara knew that the Casualty Officer didn't sit beside sick patients, and she told herself she was delirious again.

It was queer, being a patient when you had been a nurse. People standing by her bed talked incautiously when her eyes were closed, and they said the same things she had heard said on so many occasions about other patients.

'She mustn't be worried.'

'Put the red screen round the bed.'

'Tell that nurse to be more quiet with the trolley.'

'Call me at once, Nurse, if the patient shows any change.'

'Has she no family?'

'No, they may not have permission to come in. The Press have already had a statement.'

She wanted to tell them then, that she had caused the accident. She suddenly remembered it all so clearly. But her eyes wouldn't open and she drifted away again.

One day she thought she saw Sue sitting by her. 'Who are you?' she asked cautiously, to test her own ability to recognise people.

But the R.S.O. had popped up from somewhere and raised his hypodermic needle in the air and she had been banished to the shadows again.

There was a day when Barbara lay staring at the reflection in the mirror, of the streaming rain on the windows. It slapped against the windows as it had that first day in Casualty, when

Margaret Knowles had been admitted.

Clearly she found herself saying, 'Only it drummed on the roof!'

There was a movement over by the chest, and the nurse, never far away, went to the door to call someone.

Adam came in, and the nurse — at a nod from him — went out, leaving the door ajar.

'Hello,' he said softly, leaning over her. 'How are you?'

He seemed changed. She racked her brains to discover how. Had his face looked so grey and haggard before? She thought she had remembered it tanned and healthy.

'I don't know,' she said carefully. 'Don't you know?'

'Your chart tells me you're improving,' he said, with one of the special encouraging smiles he reserved for scared old patients and panicky children.

'Will I walk again?' she managed.

'Yes, indeed you will. The R.S.O. told me so!'

It was too hearty, too reassuring, but she persevered. 'Is my face hurt?'

'Not in the least!'

'But there was blood all over it when I fell down the bank,' she told him. 'I'd been trying to open the door but he locked his door and said it locked all the others!'

His wide encouraging smile fled, and a wary, alert look replaced it. 'Why would he do that?' he asked softly.

'Because I tried to jump out,' she said, simply.

It was clear that he thought she was wandering again.

'No, Adam, don't go away!' she cried, her voice rising. 'I know what I'm talking about! He was going to take me — somewhere — I didn't want to go — I tried to get away — '

'Sh-h!' he said, holding one of her hands in a firm grasp. 'You mustn't get upset or I shall have to give you another jab.'

With surprise she realised that her hands were no longer bandaged. 'Don't you want to know what happened?' she asked dully.

'Yes, if you promise not to get upset.'

'Sue said it was you calling me up, but it couldn't have been. No, I remember now — he said he could act — no, he mimicked your voice and said he was an actor — that's it! He said if I . . . went with him . . . just once . . . he'd let me go. Didn't want him! Told him to turn back — begged him to — he wouldn't listen so I grabbed the wheel — '

'Hush, hush, it's all right. It's all over,' Adam soothed her, but there was a very odd look on his face.

'You don't believe me, do you?' she said.

'I think you're remembering something that happened at some other time,' he said at last. He had that look about him that suggested he was about to go. She panicked.

'Adam, don't go! I want to know — '

Her feverish hands felt automatically for the chain she wore round her neck.

'It's not there! My ring!' she cried.

'We took the chain off, my dear. It's safe. And I've taken my ring back. I thought you'd rather. You see, there's no need any more to feel tied to me. Margaret is officially engaged to her plastic surgeon. So you see, it all worked out all right.'

'You took it back?' she whispered.

'Yes, my dear. Why didn't you tell me you were already wearing his ring? If we hadn't seen it, I would never have known!'

She shook her head. She was tired now, but it was essential that she made him understand. 'It's *my* ring,' she muttered. 'My ring.'

'Yes, I know. But when someone found you, all alone and terribly injured, lying half down that bank,' he began, but she broke in excitedly.

'You mean they didn't bring me in at the same time as Damien?' She grasped his arm. 'They must have taken Damien away because I saw them running towards the car, but I was thrown out! Don't you see?'

Her fingers bit into his wrist as she explained, and at last made him realise that the man she had been so feverishly talking about, in the car, had been Damien.

'But my dear, I thought you were engaged to Eldridge, and that it was some other fellow in the car,' he said at last, still not understanding. 'That ring you were wearing, wasn't that his ring?'

'No, no, it was my aunt's — the one she left me. It was all she left me, and I treasured it.' She thought about his explanation. 'But where is Damien? I don't want him — I hate him — but don't you see, I might have killed him, doing what I did! You said he was in this hospital!'

'No, my dearest, I said no such thing! You kept calling his name, and asking if he were going to die, and I said no — naturally! I didn't even know he'd been injured. He must have been taken to some other hospital. It was only you they brought in — only you, looking so

355

small and frail in that ambulance.' His voice broke, and he held her hands to his lips. She could feel his lips trembling against her flesh.

'Adam, I'd just like to know he's going to get better,' she faltered, 'so I can forget him. Not have him on my conscience. I don't know what it was all about. I just want to push the whole thing away into the background.'

He looked surprised. He had forgotten she didn't know the truth behind those two ugly rumours that had circulated around her. 'It was someone called Romany Tragman,' he said, slowly. Briefly he told her about the porter recognising the photograph in the film magazine, and of how Margaret had telephoned the studios and Buck Tragman had been so angry.

'Oh, now I begin to see,' she murmured. 'That explains why Buck beat Damien up. There was a time, at that horrid party, when Damien took me out by way of the back stairs. Buck went down another way, got there before us, and waited for us. Then he looked all confused when he recognised me. I remembered thinking then — *he believed Damien had come down the back stairs with his wife.*'

She managed a small smile. 'I used to be film-struck but not any more. Not after meeting those people. They were all so artificial, ready to do anything to keep on the right side of Buck Tragman, just to get a film part. That's all they cared about. I don't want to meet any of them again, ever.'

'I thought you liked Eldridge so much!'

'I know you did, and I couldn't make you see that I didn't, could I?' She looked at his hands, enclosing her small one in a grip that hurt. 'He was so angry to think I was engaged to you, without telling him. He wanted to punish me for that. And to think it was only a pretend engagement!'

'It needn't be,' he murmured brokenly.

'What did you say, Adam?'

'I cherished the hope that we might be able to keep on with it so long that you'd get used to it, so that it wouldn't be a pretend one any longer.'

'You don't know what you're saying!' she said, after giving thought to the matter. 'You're a confirmed bachelor. Once bitten, twice shy, they say! You might not like being engaged to me. Won't you be afraid of being let down again?'

'It's a chance I have to take,' he said, huskily, but managing a small smile. 'I only know I don't want to live through these last few weeks again. I thought I'd lost you, and even when they found you, every day I felt you were slipping away from me. I suppose I've loved you, Bar, since I first saw you that day in Casualty,' he said, smothering her hands with kisses.

'Oh, Adam! Can't you — don't you want to cuddle me?'

'I'm afraid of hurting you. You're still not out of the wood yet!'

'When will I be? All I've wanted is for

you to take me in your arms! It's going to be so much harder now, to wait!'

He very gently slid an arm under her, and kissed her mouth. 'My dearest, are you sure you're doing the right thing — choosing me instead of a film star? I'm not much good at this sort of thing, you know. I'm really only good at Casualty, and you know you hate that! You were only living for the day you'd be transferred to some other department. Are you sure you want to be tied for life to a Casualty Officer?'

She touched his face with one finger, caressingly. 'I told you — I'm sick of film stars. As for Casualty Officers, I only know one, and he might not be so bad in private life, just as a husband!'

We do hope that you have enjoyed reading this large print book.

Did you know that all of our titles are available for purchase?

We publish a wide range of high quality large print books including:
Romances, Mysteries, Classics
General Fiction
Non Fiction and Westerns

Special interest titles available in large print are:
The Little Oxford Dictionary
Music Book, Song Book
Hymn Book, Service Book

Also available from us courtesy of Oxford University Press:
Young Readers' Dictionary
(large print edition)
Young Readers' Thesaurus
(large print edition)

For further information or a free brochure, please contact us at:
Ulverscroft Large Print Books Ltd.,
The Green, Bradgate Road, Anstey,
Leicester, LE7 7FU, England.
Tel: (00 44) **0116 236 4325**
Fax: (00 44) **0116 234 0205**

GIRL ON THE RUN

Rhonda Baxter

A job in a patent law firm is a far cry from the glamorous existence of a pop star's girlfriend. But it's just what Jane Porter needs to distance herself from her cheating ex and the ensuing press furore. In a new city with a new look, Jane sets about rebuilding her confidence — something she intends to do alone. That is, until she meets patent lawyer Marshall Winfield. But with the paparazzi still hot on Jane's heels, and an office troublemaker hell-bent on making things difficult, can they find happiness together?